"Why D
This Was

"I didn't think it was necessary," Carina said.

"You could have warned me, at least. I practically leaped on you." Jude frowned.

She smiled. "I thought it was great."

"Well—" he looked down at her "—I'm glad you think so, but I should have taken more time with you. I was too rough, too eager. I wanted you so badly."

"You made it a marvelous experience for me."

"I thought that since you were—I mean, you were engaged, so it seemed reasonable that you had, uh, that you had—" He sighed, looking glum.

"You know, I understand there are men who actually want to be the first one with a woman."

He took a deep breath and sighed. "Probably. It's more important to me that I be the last one."

Dear Reader,

Thank you for choosing Silhouette Desire. As always, we have a fabulous array of stories for you to enjoy, starting with *Just a Taste* by Bronwyn Jameson, the latest installment in our DYNASTIES: THE ASHTONS continuity series. This tale of forbidden attraction between two romance-wary souls will leave you breathless and wanting more from this wonderful author—who will have a brand-new miniseries of her own, PRINCES OF THE OUTBACK, out later this year.

The terrific Annette Broadrick is back with another book in her CRENSHAWS OF TEXAS series. *Double Identity* is an engrossing page-turner about seduction and lies...you know, all that good stuff! Susan Crosby continues her BEHIND CLOSED DOORS series with *Rules of Attraction*, the first of three brand-new stories set in the world of very private investigations. Roxanne St. Claire brings us a fabulous McGrath brother hero caught in an unexpected situation, in *When the Earth Moves*. Rochelle Alers's THE BLACKSTONES OF VIRGINIA series wraps up with *Beyond Business*, a story in which the Blackstone patriarch gets involved in a surprise romance with his new—and very pregnant—assistant. And last but certainly not least, the engaging Amy Jo Cousins is back this month with *Sleeping Arrangements*, a terms-of-the-will story not to be missed.

Here's hoping you enjoy all six of our selections this month. And, in the months to come, look for Maureen Child's THREE-WAY WAGER series and a brand-new installment of our infamous TEXAS CATTLEMAN'S CLUB.

Happy reading!

Melissa Jeglinski

Melissa Jeglinski
Senior Editor
Silhouette Desire

Please address questions and book requests to:
Silhouette Reader Service
U.S.: 3010 Walden Ave., P.O. Box 1325, Buffalo, NY 14269
Canadian: P.O. Box 609, Fort Erie, Ont. L2A 5X3

ANNETTE BROADRICK

DOUBLE IDENTITY

Published by Silhouette Books
America's Publisher of Contemporary Romance

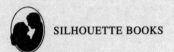 SILHOUETTE BOOKS

ISBN 0-373-76646-7

DOUBLE IDENTITY

Copyright © 2005 by Annette Broadrick

Visit Silhouette Books at www.eHarlequin.com

Printed in U.S.A.

ANNETTE BROADRICK

believes in romance and the magic of life. Since 1984, Annette has shared her view of life and love with readers. In addition to being nominated by *Romantic Times* as one of the Best New Authors of that year, she has also won the *Romantic Times* Reviewers' Choice Award for Best in its Series, the *Romantic Times* WISH Award; and the *Romantic Times* Lifetime Achievement Awards for Series Romance and Series Romantic Fantasy.

One

Jude Crenshaw's phone rang at seven o'clock, waking him from a deep, exhausted sleep at his condo in Fort Meade, Maryland. He fumbled for the phone without opening his eyes.

"Crenshaw," he mumbled.

"This is Ms. Kincaid's office calling. One moment, please." He was put on hold. Kincaid was his supervisor at the National Security Agency.

Jude had worked for the agency for the past four years. He'd been hired as a civilian after leaving the army, where he'd been in Special Ops. He had been in the field until six months ago when he'd been promoted to a supervisory position.

He couldn't imagine why Jackie Kincaid would be calling him at home at this time of morning. He sat up, rubbed his hand over his face and swung his legs to the floor.

"Jude? Jackie. Sorry to bother you so early. I tried to reach you yesterday, but you must have been incommunicado. I couldn't get my calls to go through on your cell phone so I could leave a message."

"I've been on the west coast for the past two weeks. Got home in the wee hours this morning."

"I know you're on vacation this week but something's come up here that needs your presence."

"Staff problems?"

"Nothing like that. We need you at an interdepartmental meeting at nine."

He frowned. "What department?"

"DEA."

"You're kidding me."

"Nope. Do you think you can get here by that time?"

Jude yawned and said, "Sure. No problem."

"Great. See you then."

Jude stood and stretched. His body was still on Pacific Standard Time, which meant he was having to function at four in the morning.

He went into his kitchen and made a pot of coffee that would be ready by the time he finished his shower. In the bathroom, his bleary-eyed gaze looked back at him from the mirror.

He needed a haircut.

He'd been out in the sun quite a bit while in southern California, so that his skin was deeply tanned and his blond hair lighter than usual.

Jude showered and shaved, dressed and returned to the kitchen for his caffeine fix. After his first cup, he filled a thermos cup with the rest of the coffee to drink on the way to work and went into the garage where he kept his baby.

His two-seater late-model Porsche spent more time in

the garage than out on the road. He'd been looking forward to a few days off so he could take her out, wind her up and put her through her paces. The car was the love of his life, and why not? She was always waiting at home when he got there, never complained about the hours he kept, didn't demand attention and didn't eat him out of house and home while he was away.

He hit the garage-door button as he stepped through the door and slid behind the wheel. When he turned on the engine, he smiled at the whisper of sound. She was purring for him.

Jude drove to the NSA office complex sipping on his coffee, determined not to let the rush-hour traffic disturb him. Once there, he went to his office, checked his mail and headed down the hall to Kincaid's office.

He stopped at the desk of Kincaid's assistant, who looked up from opening the morning mail and saw him.

"Welcome back, Blue Eyes," Justine said, her expression mischievous. "I like the tan. Wish I had nothing better to do than lie around on a beach all day soaking up some rays."

He lifted one eyebrow and said, "Yeah, me, too. I have an appointment with Jackie."

"Go right in. Mm-mm. I swear, that tan shows you off quite nicely. You probably have to fight off all the women you meet."

He shook his head and grinned. "Not so's you'd notice."

Justine was in her midthirties, happily married with three young daughters. She'd teased him ever since she'd met him that he'd be her pick for a son-in-law if he'd only wait to find a bride until her daughters were grown.

He tapped on Jackie's door and walked inside.

Three men and a woman sat in front of Jackie's desk. They turned to look at him, their faces grim.

One of the men stood and turned to face Jude.

He looked to be in his late forties, possibly early fifties, with thick dark hair liberally sprinkled with gray. The man looked trim, probably worked out several times each week. His eyes missed nothing about Jude and Jude caught himself before he polished his shoe on the back of his pants leg.

"Jude, this is Sam Watson from the Drug Enforcement Agency. With him are three of his agents: John Greene, Hal Pennington and Ruth Littlefield." The agents stood and Jude shook hands with each of them.

"Now that we're all here, let's go into the conference room where we'll have a little more room," Jackie said, and led the way out of her office.

Once they were seated around the conference table, Jackie said, "Sam, I'll let you explain to Jude why you wanted to see him."

Watson smiled, transforming his craggy face, and Jude decided that the man was younger than he appeared at first glance.

"Thanks, Jackie," Watson replied. He turned to Jude. "I have a major problem with my San Antonio office at the moment. One of my men was killed last week and we have reason to believe that another agent was responsible."

Jude straightened. "Damn. That's really tough." He glanced at the other agents. "You've got to trust the man who's got your back."

If possible, they looked even grimmer as each one nodded.

"I need to get someone down there who I can trust and who can go undercover for us. In my search, I came across your file. You've worked covert operations for several years."

"That's true."

"And you're from Texas."

Jude grinned. "Can't deny that, either."

"I also found out that your family is well-known in Texas."

"Well, there's a lot of us there, I'll admit."

"You would be ideal for what I want to do."

Jude nodded and waited.

"Here's the deal. For the past several months we've been investigating a family by the name of Patterson. They own an import/export business which we believe they're using to smuggle arms, drugs and an assortment of contraband into the United States.

"Gregg, the agent who died, was one of several working to obtain evidence against the Pattersons because we need to get them behind bars as quickly as possible, especially now that we think they bribed an agent or two to look the other way. The Pattersons seem to be one step ahead of us no matter what we plan, so it's obvious they're getting their information from somewhere inside our group. We've made raids and found nothing and we're being accused of harassing honest businessmen."

Watson paused and poured some water from a pitcher nearby into a glass. Once he'd drunk some, he continued.

"Two days before he died, Gregg skipped the chain of command and contacted me on his own. He said he was suspicious of two of the other agents. He felt the investigation had turned up some important information that had not been passed on. He told me he planned to find out what was going on. I told him to call me as soon as he found out. That was the last time I heard from him. A few days later he was killed in an automobile accident."

"Sounds like somebody figured out that he'd reported to you."

"That's my take on the matter. I pretended to believe that Gregg's death was an accident and told the local agents to drop the investigation for lack of evidence, so the Pattersons must feel they're working in the clear now."

Jude frowned. "Where do I fit into this?"

"We need someone we can trust who is trained in undercover work to keep the investigation going. John, Hal and Ruth are from our Virginia office and they'll be your team. They aren't known to anyone in the San Antonio office and they'll be working with you to find out who killed Gregg.

"What we need is someone who can get close to the family without raising suspicion. When I discovered your background, your impressive record and your family's reputation, I asked Jackie if I could borrow you for the next several months to work for us."

Jude scratched his chin. "It's been a few months since I did any undercover work."

"I doubt that you've forgotten much. You were damned good at what you did."

"If I understand correctly, you want me to go to San Antonio as myself, get involved with the Patterson family and find evidence of illegal activities."

"Yes."

"Do you have any idea how I'm supposed to get close to them?"

"As a matter of fact, I do. The Patterson family includes a twenty-five-year-old daughter who happens to be single. We want you to arrange to meet her and ask her out. If you two start dating, the rest of the family will grow used to seeing you around and won't be suspicious of you."

"You want me to *date* her?"

"Correct."

"What if she isn't interested in dating me?"

"Oh, with your charm, good looks and the added benefit of being from a well-known Texas family, I think she'll be interested enough to accept a date with you. After that, you'll have to play it by ear. The more often you see her, the better."

Jude looked at Jackie and then at the other three. He noticed that Ruth looked amused. "I may have good covert skills but I'm lacking in the charm-and-good-looks part. I'm not what anyone would call a ladies' man."

Watson replied, "Guess you'd better learn, because that's going to be your cover when you move there. We've rented a large house for the four of you while you're there. It's in a gated community with good security."

Jude studied his hands. "So I'm supposed to be a ladies' man, huh?"

"You'll be a free-wheeling playboy with too much time on his hands. Get a reputation for being seen with beautiful women and get involved in the arts."

Jude straightened. "The arts? Are you kidding me?"

"The daughter—her name is Carina—is a pianist. She was in her third year of study at Juilliard when her father fell ill, so she returned to Texas, rented an apartment in San Antonio and plans to finish school in another year.

"You need to show an interest in music, donate money to worthy causes and figure out the best way to approach her. Developing a close friendship with her is crucial if we're going to put them behind bars."

"Is she part of the smuggling?"

"Hard to tell at this point. She could be. Part of your job will be to find out. I'm convinced we can make this work."

Jude nodded. "All right, if you think I can help, I'll do my best."

"Good," Sam said, standing up. Jackie, Jude and the

agents stood, as well. Watson placed his briefcase on the table, opened it and handed Jude a fat file. "Here are the dossiers on each member of the family."

Jude picked up the file. "When do you want me to start?"

Sam smiled sardonically. "Yesterday?"

Jude nodded. "Gotcha."

Two

Six Months Later

He spotted her as soon as she walked into the ballroom.

Carina Patterson was petite. For tonight's benefit for the San Antonio Symphony she'd chosen to wear a short, flame-red dress, sleeveless with a mandarin collar, the color in stark contrast to her fair skin and dark hair. Her lipstick matched the dress, emphasizing a sultry mouth.

She was more beautiful in person than in the several photographs he had of her. He watched as she spoke to some of the guests. Studying her, he realized that her beauty was enhanced by her vivacious manner and sparkling smile.

He enjoyed watching her walk across the room. She had a rhythm about her as though she moved to the sound of music that only she could hear.

Jude stood near the open bar with several of the movers and shakers of San Antonio society and listened with half an ear to their conversation. He glanced around the room, which glittered from the expensive chandeliers and the jewelry that adorned the women attending the benefit. The murmur of voices filled the room, drowning out the soft music being played by a small orchestra.

"Jude, we can't thank you enough for what you've done tonight for the symphony," Graham Scott, San Antonio's mayor, said. "They've been struggling to survive for a long while."

"I'm pleased to see such a strong turnout," Jude replied. "With the proceeds from tonight's tickets as well as the merchandise donated for the silent auctions, the symphony should have enough money to cover their operating costs for the coming year."

"When we first discussed this benefit," Glenn Kingston, one of the businessmen in the group, said, "we knew we'd have to deduct the cost of the event from ticket sales. Because of your generosity, all the money raised will be available for operating costs. We owe you a great debt of appreciation, Crenshaw."

Jude grinned. "Don't worry. I can afford it."

The other three men laughed at his matter-of-fact statement. Of course he could afford it. He was a Crenshaw of Texas, after all.

Since arriving in San Antonio, he'd diligently built up his image as a rich and rather indolent playboy. He'd made the rounds of art shows, museum functions and symphony performances. He'd made certain that he was seen with a beautiful woman, always a different one, at each of the functions, which quite often put his face in the society section of the paper.

His reputation was now in full swing. Not one of these

men had much respect for his lifestyle. Oh, they played the political game. Each man knew that he didn't want to get crossways with a Crenshaw, even if this particular one didn't have much ambition. So he was received everywhere, including the country club where he played golf with several members.

Now it was time to make his move.

Jude continued to watch Carina as she moved toward her assigned table. He noticed that a couple already seated were waiting there for her, and he recognized her parents. He waited for a lull in the conversation around him before he casually asked the group, "Who's the dark-haired woman in the red dress?" He nodded toward Carina.

Clint Jackson, a city councilman, answered. "Her name is Carina Patterson. She's the only daughter of Christopher Patterson. Chris and his wife, Connie, rarely attend social events. I'm pleased to see them here."

Jude pretended to think for a moment. "The name means nothing to me. Who is he?"

"Before his stroke a couple of years ago, he was quite active in the community. He imports merchandise from around the world, such as antique furniture, rugs, marble figurines, that sort of thing. Because of his health, he turned the business over to his sons, Alfred and Ben."

Jude deliberately focused on the three people sitting across the room before he turned to the group and said, "Carina looks like her mother. They have an exotic look about them."

Clint responded by saying, "Connie Patterson comes from a wealthy family in Mexico City. I understand that Chris took one look at her and fell in love."

"I can understand why," Jude responded with a grin. "She looks more like Carina's sister than her mother. Carina is truly stunning. Do you know if she's seeing someone?"

"I don't think so," Clint said. "Just in case you're thinking of making a move in that direction, here's a friendly warning, okay? Al and Ben, who are several years older than Carina, are highly protective of her. They wouldn't take kindly to someone hurting their sister in any way."

"You don't think I meet their standards?" Jude asked with amusement.

"I didn't say that," Clint said with a chuckle. "You're a Crenshaw, after all. However, you do have a reputation around town of playing the field. Let's face it, Jude, you're a great catch for any woman and they tend to throw themselves at you." He grinned. "My wife thinks you've got movie-star looks as well as charisma. I have to take her word for it since you're just not my type."

Jude laughed. "That's good to know."

"The thing is, if Al or Ben thought you were leading Carina on, there'd be hell to pay."

"Duly noted. Now would you introduce me to them?"

"Sure." As they walked across the room, Clint added, "I can see that you don't scare off very easily."

"I don't scare off at all."

Several people stopped them along the way, thanking Jude for his generous contribution to the symphony. He smiled, shook hands with them and thanked them for coming. When they finally reached the Patterson table, Jude saw that Carina's brothers and their wives had joined the group.

Clint said, "Good evening, Chris," and offered his hand to the older man. "I'm so pleased to see you here."

Patterson lifted his left hand and clasped Clint's hand. "Wouldn't have missed it for the world," he said gruffly.

"I'd like you to meet Jude Crenshaw. I understand he twisted a few arms for donations to the silent auction in order to make certain tonight was a success." He turned to

Jude. "Jude, it gives me great pleasure to introduce Christopher Patterson, his lovely wife, Connie, his daughter, Carina, his son, Alfred, and Al's wife, Marisa, and his son, Ben, and Ben's wife, Sara."

Here was a stroke of luck Jude hadn't expected. Meeting the entire family was well worth the money and time he'd spent on tonight's benefit. In addition, his contribution was truly for a good cause.

"I'm pleased to meet each one of you," he said, shaking hands.

Carina looked up at him. "Thank you for tonight," she said in a husky voice.

"You're quite welcome, Ms. Patterson." Their eyes met and he winked at her. She looked a little startled at first and then grinned at him.

So far, so good.

From the corner of his eye, he caught Al watching them closely. Without appearing to notice, Jude turned away. He and Clint returned to the bar, refreshed their drinks, and went to the head table.

Dinner was first-class and the speeches were mercifully short, for which Jude was thankful.

The orchestra changed from playing quiet dinner music to show tunes to encourage dancing. Jude excused himself from his table and crossed the room to the Pattersons. The only ones there were Mr. and Mrs. Patterson.

"Mr. Patterson, may I have your permission to ask your wife to dance? I promise not to run off with her afterwards, although I'll admit the idea is tempting."

Patterson chuckled. "Of course you can. Just remember that I saw her first."

Jude turned to Connie Patterson and saw that she was blushing. "May I have this dance?"

She nodded, and Jude held out his hand. She took it and gracefully rose from the table. Once on the dance floor she said, "You helped make tonight a success, Mr. Crenshaw. We all are quite grateful." He heard a slight accent in her voice.

He smiled in acknowledgement and said, "Please, call me Jude."

"If you'll call me Connie."

"Thank you. You're a very good dancer, by the way."

Her smile held a hint of sadness. "Chris and I used to dance a great deal before his stroke. I know he misses dancing as much as I do. You were kind to offer."

"Believe me, it's my pleasure." The orchestra segued into another song with a similar beat. "Will your husband be all right on his own a little longer?"

She glanced toward the table and smiled. "He's not alone. Carina has returned to the table."

They finished the dance and walked back to where Carina and her father sat watching them.

Patterson was the first to speak. "You look wonderful out there, dear," he said to Connie. "Please enjoy this opportunity and don't worry about me."

She sank into the chair beside him. "I'm too out of breath to dance any more at the moment." She smiled at Jude. "Thank you again."

"You're quite welcome." He turned his gaze to Carina. "Ms. Patterson, may I have this dance with you?"

She glanced at her mother's radiant face and said, "Yes."

Once she stood he took her hand, led her to the dance floor and took her in his arms. She was smaller than her mother. Her head barely came to his shoulder. She was delicately boned and she reminded him of a Dresden figurine—fragile and exquisite.

"It was kind of you to ask my mother to dance. She doesn't get out very much."

"She mentioned that she and your father used to love to dance."

She nodded, her eyes glistening. "Yes. They were something to watch—so graceful and talented. They moved as one. I know they both must miss it terribly."

After a moment, he asked, "When did he have his stroke?"

"Two years ago. He'd always been so active and healthy that none of us were prepared for his sudden illness. There were a few days when we weren't certain he would pull through, but he has a very strong will. He's done everything he could to keep his body as toned as possible."

In his most casual tone, Jude said, "I understand he has a thriving business in imports."

"My brothers are in charge now. They keep him informed about the business, which has actually grown under their management."

"He must be relieved to be able to depend on them."

"He never talks about his infirmity. He's very matter of fact about being in his motorized wheelchair." She glanced over at her table. "We're all very proud of him."

"How about you? Do you get out very often?"

She smiled ruefully. "Not really, no."

"Would you make an exception for me?"

She looked at him in surprise. "You're asking me out?"

"Yes, I am. Like every man here, I noticed you as soon as you walked in tonight. I'll admit I coaxed Clint into introducing you and your family to me. I'd really like to see you again."

The song ended and another one began. He continued to dance and she made no comment about wanting to return to her table.

"What did you have in mind?" she finally asked.

He burst into laughter. "Now there's a loaded question if I ever heard one. My intentions are quite innocent, I assure you. I thought we could have dinner some evening, perhaps next Saturday, if you're available."

She seemed to relax a little. "That sounds innocuous enough."

"I swear on my Boy Scout honor that you will be safe with me."

He led her into a couple of turns, which she followed like a pro.

"You dance very well," she said with a smile.

"Thanks. My mom would be proud to hear you say that. I wasn't one of her best pupils, but I manage to get by."

She tilted her head slightly and asked, "Are you a musician, by any chance? You have a natural rhythm, like most musicians."

He laughed. "'Fraid not. The only instrument I play is the radio."

She groaned. "And yet you support the arts," she pointed out.

"I'm not a priest, and yet I support the church."

She laughed, a glissando of musical sound he found delightful. "Good point."

The music stopped and the orchestra took a break. Jude took the opportunity to say, "Why don't you give me your phone number? I'll call you later in the week."

She reached into the minuscule purse that hung from the tie at her waist. "Here's my card. That has my home phone and cell phone, as well. I spend my Saturdays with my parents, so you'll need to pick me up at their place."

"I can do that." As he helped her into her seat, he leaned near her ear and said, "I'm looking forward to seeing you again." He straightened and spoke to Chris and Connie. "I'm very pleased to have met each of you. I hope to see you again."

They responded in a friendly manner and he walked away.

By the time the evening ended, Jude was more than ready to go home.

He spoke to several people on his way to his sports car. Once he negotiated San Antonio's downtown streets, he reached the highway and headed north. The house the agency had rented was located in the hills north of the city, and had a scenic view of the Hill Country.

He could reach the family ranch in a couple of hours, although he hadn't been to see them very often. They knew he was working an undercover assignment and gave him the space he needed. He missed them, though. He'd have to get up there soon.

Jude turned off the highway and followed the snakelike road up through the hills until he reached the summit. The house was surrounded by a thick, stucco six-foot wall. Once there, Jude keyed in the security numbers for the day and waited until the gate opened, then followed the curving driveway up to the house and parked in the three-car garage. He noted the other cars were there. The agents were probably asleep by now. He knew he was more than ready to hit the sack.

Once inside, he went to the den where a large screen projected the various scenes shown by hidden cameras located throughout the property. Their team had several computers at work in the room…one collecting data, another running probabilities and another waiting instructions.

Jude picked up the phone and tapped in a series of numbers. His call was answered on the first ring. Without waiting for a voice, Jude said, "I made contact tonight. Looks like we're in."

Three

Jude opened the file containing information on the Patterson family. The files were so detailed that he probably knew more about them than they knew about each other.

He knew that forty-two-year-old Alfredo de la Cruz Patterson kept a mistress in Houston and paid for her penthouse condominium.

He knew that Benito spent much of his time out of the country, ostensibly selling and buying merchandise. Jude needed to find out exactly what he was buying and from whom.

He hoped the brothers were the only ones involved in the smuggling activities and that the rest of the family wasn't aware of what they were doing. It would be a shame to arrest Christopher Patterson for aiding and abetting as well as obstructing justice.

Jude stood and stretched. He turned off the light and

went upstairs to bed, feeling good about what he'd accomplished so far. He'd finally made contact and Carina had accepted his invitation to go out with him.

The following Thursday morning Carina met her sister-in-law Marisa for coffee at one of their favorite bakeries.

"Thanks for calling me to meet you this morning," Marisa said. "I need someone I trust that I can talk to."

"Trouble with Al?" Carina asked, sipping her coffee.

"It seems that's all we have anymore. I'm thinking about divorcing him."

Carina reached out and placed her hand over Marisa's hand. "It's gotten that bad, has it?"

"He's been ignoring me for the last several months, which is upsetting enough, but now he's ignoring the children, as well. It breaks my heart to see them wanting his attention while he brushes them off."

Six-year-old Chris was the first grandchild and had been named for his grandfather. His sister, Tina Maria, was a precocious four-year-old. Carina loved them, as she loved Ben and Sara's daughter, Beth. She knew they were each a handful and needed both parents.

"I think there's another woman," Marisa said in a low voice.

"Oh, surely not," Carina replied. "What makes you think such a thing?"

"He's been going on what he insists are 'buying trips,' which is something he's always left to Benito before. Sara says that as far as she knows, Bennie does most of the buying for the company. I've been thinking about hiring an investigator."

"Be careful," Carina said. "Alfredo has a temper. I wouldn't want him to hurt you in any way."

"I told him last night that I wanted a divorce and he just laughed and asked if I was trying to get a higher allowance for household expenses. He refuses to take me seriously."

"But what would you do if you found out there was someone else?"

Marisa sighed. "Accept that I really don't have much of a marriage and that the kids and I need to go somewhere else. My mother keeps wanting me to go visit her in Dallas for a while and I'm thinking seriously of doing just that."

"I want to see you and the kids happy, Marisa. I feel bad that I'm the one who introduced you to him."

Marisa smiled, her first smile since they'd met that morning. "Hey, you didn't force me to marry him, you know. I made that decision all on my own." She took a bite out of her pastry. "I'm sorry to dump all this on you just because you're my friend. You're also Alfredo's sister. I don't want you caught in the middle here."

"Don't be silly. You and I have been friends since high school. Nothing's going to change that, not even a divorce."

"Don't say anything to the folks until I make a decision. I think getting away is just what I need to give myself some time to think about things. I'm glad school's out for the summer. It may be that I'll start Chris in school in Dallas for next year."

"You do what you need to do, Marisa. Just remember, I'm here for you." Carina looked away for a moment before she said, "Neither of us did too well in the men department, did we?"

"At least you knew Dan loved you."

"Of course he did. That's why he had a woman with him the night he was killed. I was such a fool to think he was in love with me and not the Patterson name. Al wouldn't have hired him if I hadn't been engaged to Dan and you know it."

"I guess you're right. All men are slimeballs and we're both better off without them," Marisa said politely with no expression on her face.

Carina laughed and Marisa joined in. After they polished off their pastries and got more coffee, Carina said, "This probably isn't a great time to mention it, but I have a date with Jude Crenshaw Saturday evening."

Marisa stared at her, her cup of coffee halfway to her mouth. She set the mug back on the table.

"You're kidding me! He asked you out?"

"Don't sound so shocked. He asked me while we were dancing at the benefit last week."

"I guess I'm more shocked that you accepted him. You've known for days and you're just now telling me about it? Boy, when you decide to start dating again, you don't mess around! Jude Crenshaw. He's one of the most talked-about bachelors in town! I can't begin to imagine how many hearts he's broken since he moved here."

Carina shook her head. "Doesn't matter. He certainly won't break mine. I've been thinking that I need to get back into some sort of social life. Since Dan died, I've hibernated in my apartment feeling sorry for myself. It's time to move on and accept the fact that I have lousy taste in men. I figure Jude will be a good first step in letting people know I'm ready to start dating again."

"I know a couple of women who've dated him. They both had the same experience with him. He saw them a few times, they hit it off, he was a fun date, rarely if ever serious about anything and they were both really taken with him. And then, for no reason that either of them could fathom, he stopped calling them. Just like that." Marisa snapped her fingers. "He gave no explanation to either one. The next thing either of them knew he was seeing someone else. He definitely believes in playing the field."

"Good. Then he's perfect for me because that's what I want to do. I admit I'm a little flattered that he even noticed me since I'm not his type. He seems to go for tall blondes. I haven't gone out with that many men and I've never been serious about anyone but Dan. I'm sadly lacking in my dating skills."

"Not to mention lack of a sex life."

Carina grinned mischievously. "That, too. I may not put up much of a defense if Mr. Crenshaw insists on seducing me."

"Come to think of it," Marisa said, sounding disgruntled, "Maybe I need to get a boyfriend on the side, then, since my sex life has all but disappeared."

They looked at each other for a moment and then burst into laughter.

Carina changed the subject and they spent the rest of their time together discussing what had gone on at the board meeting of the symphony the night before. Carina had been on the board since she'd returned from New York after her father became ill.

After a while, Marisa glanced at her watch. "Oops. Time to pick up the kiddos. Be sure to let me know how your date goes, okay?" They stood and walked toward the door of the small bakery.

"I'll do that, and say hi to the kids."

Marisa sighed. "Of course." They paused once they were on the sidewalk. "You know, Carina, there are times when I don't feel I even know Al any more. He's certainly not the man I married."

Carina gently squeezed her hand. "Hang in there. I know you'll make the best decision for all concerned."

* * *

Carina dressed for her dinner with Jude on Saturday wondering how the evening would go. Would he find her too boring for words?

Carina sank down onto her bed and smoothed the hand-stitched coverlet her grandmother in Mexico had made for her several years ago. She closed her eyes and visualized Jude with his blond, expensively styled hair and those gorgeous blue eyes.

He was much taller than she. Danny had only been a couple of inches taller when she wore high heels. Even in her highest heels, she had barely reached Jude's shoulder.

He'd been so gentle with her, almost as if he'd thought she might break. If he got to know her better, he'd quickly discover that she was far from fragile. She kept her body strong and supple with tai chi and yoga.

Of course he was handsome. And rich. And something of a playboy. But did she care about his playing the field? She'd told Marisa the truth. She wasn't looking for a long-term relationship.

Carina glanced at her watch. Jude would be here soon and she didn't want to keep him waiting. For all she knew, he might decide not to wait for her. He probably had a list of women's names he could call at the last minute if he chose to leave. She smiled at the thought. I wonder if my name will be added to that list?

Jude stopped his car in front of the gate to the grounds of the Patterson property, located in the Alamo Heights district of San Antonio. Some of these mansions had been in the same family for generations, so he wasn't too surprised to discover that the Pattersons' home was here.

He pushed the button on the security box and a male voice immediately spoke. "Identification, please."

"Jude Crenshaw, here to see Carina Patterson."

There was a pause and then the double wrought-iron gates swung open. He drove through and followed the curving driveway up an incline to the front of the house.

The Pattersons' compound took up the entire block. Jude noted two other houses situated nearby. Guest houses, he presumed. The estate was almost large enough to hold a golf course!

He parked in front of the antebellum-style home and got out. Before he reached the top of the three shallow steps to the veranda, one of the double doors swung open. The man who stood there looked more like a former cop than a butler.

"Good evening, Mr. Crenshaw," the man said. "Carina is in the music room. Follow the hallway past the stairs and enter the first door on your right."

The foyer was wide and ran the entire length of the house. The staircase rose in a graceful curve to the second floor. Jude glanced up, past the second-floor landing at the ceiling and saw a multi-beveled glass dome that let in light.

When he reached the indicated door, Jude saw Carina seated at a piano, playing, her back him. He stood listening to her. Because her file had noted her passion for music, he'd immersed himself in classical music by attending concerts for the past several months. He was impressed by her skills, despite the fact that he much preferred country-and-western music.

Now he was known as a patron of the arts.

He doubted very much if his dad or his three brothers would believe that he'd actually come to appreciate the skill, practice and talent needed to play a musical instrument that wasn't a guitar.

One of the walls had floor-to-ceiling windows that looked out over a lush garden, making a colorful backdrop to the grand piano and the musician. He waited until she finished the song and then clapped his hands in appreciation. Carina's head swung around in surprise and she rose from the piano. "Jude, please forgive me for being so rude. Helmuth didn't tell me you were here and I'm afraid I lose all track of time when I'm playing."

She walked toward him, wearing a cool-looking sleeveless dress that matched the green of her eyes.

"Then I can only thank Helmuth for the oversight," he replied, "because I would have missed hearing you play just now. You take my breath away… I mean, your playing…" He stopped, knowing that he would only dig a hole for himself by attempting to clarify his comment.

Jude took her hands in his. "You have such small hands to be able to make such beautiful music."

"Believe me, I wish they were larger. I've had to compensate for my lack of reach over the keyboard all my life."

"If you're ready, shall we go?"

When they reached the front entrance he saw that Helmuth hovered by the door. Carina paused in front of him. "Jude, I'd like you to meet Helmuth Gregorian. Helmuth has been with our family since before I was born."

Jude held out his hand. "Good to meet you."

Helmuth shook his hand and nodded. A man of few words, obviously.

When Carina saw his car, her eyes widened. "Oh, my. That's quite a car you have there, Mr. Crenshaw."

"Jude. My name is Jude."

"How long have you had it?" she asked, as he opened

the passenger door and helped her inside. He closed the door and walked around to the other side. Once he started the car, he replied.

"A couple of years, now."

"It looks brand new. You must take good care of it."

He grinned. "One of my many vices."

Once he reached the end of the driveway and turned onto the street, Jude glanced at her and said, "I made reservations for us at a place north of town with a nice view. We'll be there in about thirty minutes. I hope that's all right with you."

She patted the butter-soft leather of the upholstery and chuckled. "Are you kidding? I could ride in this for weeks."

"That's good to know. So if I decide to kidnap you one of these days, does that mean you won't put up much of a struggle?"

"Well," she said slowly, "that would depend on why you'd kidnapped me."

"Oh, rest assured it would be for nefarious purposes."

"Well, in that case," she said, laughing, "I probably wouldn't mind."

She leaned back in her seat and appeared to relax, which was good. First dates were always tough. Add to that his motive for taking her out…and the evening became even tougher.

They rode along in silence while Jude traversed the various streets that he could swear had originally been cow paths from the way they meandered through the city.

Once on the expressway, Carina said, "Tell me something about yourself, Jude. All I know is that you're a native Texan and that you're a member of the well-known Crenshaw family."

Reasonable question. He'd stick to the truth as much as possible, with the exception of his playboy image.

"There's not much to tell and what there is you'll find boring. I'm thirty years old. I enjoy being outdoors and can't imagine myself working in an office all day." That was true enough.

"Where were you born? Where did you go to school? Tell me something about your family. Why did you invite me for dinner?"

He laughed. "The last one's easy. Because I'm attracted to you and want to get to know you better." He teased her by saying, "Why is it I feel as though I'm being interviewed? Will I read about myself in tomorrow's paper?"

She laughed. "Oh, no. They'd never get an article into print that fast. Probably some time next week."

"Oh. Well then, I suppose that's all right." They headed out of the city and the traffic thinned out a little before he spoke. "I was born in a little town you've probably never heard of, New Eden, which is located about a hundred miles northwest of here. My family's been there since the 1840s, when one of my ancestors arrived in Texas and bought land in the Hill Country. My dad is the oldest of four brothers and he has four sons."

"Oh, my. Did his brothers have that many children?"

"Not quite. My uncle Jeffrey has two sons, Jordan and Jackson. Uncle Josh has three sons: Jeremy, Justin and James, and Uncle Jerome has three sons: Jed, Jesse and Johnny."

"Whew. That's a lot of people with names starting with *J.* And what's with the all-male households?"

"Well, there were women born to some of our ancestors, but not many. And my oldest brother, Jake, broke the cycle by producing a little girl—Heather—a few years ago."

"Tell me about your brothers."

Watson had been right. His background would hold up to any scrutiny if someone was checking on him because it wasn't part of his cover.

He relaxed a little more and said, "Let's see. Jake is almost thirty-four. He's the rancher in our family. He married the foreman's daughter, Ashley, last fall and they're expecting their first child together any time now. Heather is from his first marriage and he has full custody of her.

"Jared, an oil geologist, got married a few weeks after Jake. He's thirty-two. I was up at the ranch earlier this month for a big barbecue my dad put on welcoming Jared back from Saudi Arabia. We were all relieved to hear he won't be going back.

"I'm the third son. My younger brother, Jason, is in Delta Force."

"Is he married?"

"Nope. He and I enjoy our freedom too much to give serious thought to settling down. At least not for several years, anyway."

"So you're definitely a native Texan."

"Yep. Went all the way through high school in New Eden and as soon as I graduated I joined the army…at the insistence of my father and the local sheriff."

"The sheriff? What had you done?"

"Nothing too serious, actually, but I guess I was heading in that direction, or so my dad thought. I ran with a couple of guys who loved to pull pranks and push the limit. Let's just say we were a little too rowdy for the small town. We'd sneak beer, race our cars down Main Street, give our teachers migraines and in general made a name for ourselves.

"My dad wasn't impressed. He was the one who strongly suggested I find something more productive to do with my life than remove street signs, decorate people's lawns with toilet paper and see who had the fastest wheels. I recall hearing the words *learn a little discipline.*"

"A delinquent, were you?" she asked with a grin.

He chuckled. "Close to it."

"Then you went into the army."

"Uh-huh."

"Then what?"

He gave her another glance before he said with a smile, "I got out of the army at the end of my enlistment and promised myself I'd never go back." His first big lie. He'd enjoyed the army and had learned a lot about himself. He'd joined Delta Force a few months after he enlisted. The army had challenged him and he discovered that he thrived on challenge. They'd paid for his college education and promoted him to officer status when he graduated. He'd moved steadily up the ranks and would probably still be in the army if the NSA hadn't approached him about working for them.

"A little too much discipline, I take it?" Carina asked.

"Something like that," he replied. "So now you know my entire life story. I warned you it would be boring."

"What made you move to San Antonio?"

"No one particular reason. My uncle Josh asked me to oversee some of the family property and businesses in the area. Since I didn't have much else to do, I decided I'd check out the area, meet some people, that kind of thing. Speaking of my uncle, he was the one who first showed me how to find the restaurant where we're going. I've been back several times since then. The food is great and the view outstanding."

They lapsed into silence for a few miles before Jude looked at her and said, "Now it's your turn. Tell me about you."

He wondered how much information she would share with him.

"Compared to you, my life has been *truly* boring."

He smiled but didn't comment.

"I was born in San Antonio, went to school here, went to college in New York for a while and moved back home. That's pretty much my story in a nutshell."

"You don't mention your music."

"Oh. My music. I suppose that's because it's such an integral part of me I don't think about it. It's like having green eyes and dark hair. Music is part of who I am."

"Do you intend to pursue a career in music?"

"I hope to. I need one more year at Juilliard to get my degree. I'm registered for this fall so I'll be going back soon."

"Good for you. Then I'm glad I met you before you moved away."

Jude waited to see if she would mention her fiancé, Daniel Bowie. According to his information, Bowie had been killed fourteen months ago in a hit-and-run accident south of San Antonio. The police report stated that he must have been traveling at a high speed when he was sideswiped. He'd lost control of his car and it had flipped several times, killing him instantly. They'd never discovered who hit him or if the collision had been intentional. The case was still open but they'd run out of leads.

He waited but she didn't say anything more. Finally, he asked, "What about brothers and sisters?"

"You met my two brothers at the benefit. Alfredo is sixteen years older than I and Benito is fourteen years older. They were already out of the house by the time I was old enough to remember them living at home. Al has taken over the role of my protector, which is a little irritating at my age. In fact, Al looks after everyone in the family. My dad was grateful that Al stepped in and took over running our business once we knew that Dad wouldn't be able to continue."

"Does your brother Ben work there, as well?"

"Yes. He's the quiet one. His wife, Sara, complains that he's always off on buying trips, but somebody has to do it and Al has enough to handle here. I'm always telling her she should go with him, but so far, she's stayed at home."

"Do you have any nieces and nephews?"

"Two nieces and a nephew. Chris and Tina Maria belong to Al and Marisa. Sara and Ben have a toddler, Beth."

"And you? Do you want to have a family?"

She didn't answer right away. Finally, she said, "I love children and I want a family, but I want to finish my studies first and see where that takes me."

"So you're footloose and fancy free, just like me."

"I'm not sure about that. I doubt that we have much in common."

He gave her a sharp look before returning his eyes to the road. "What makes you say that?"

"From everything I've heard about you, you lead a busy social life. Whenever your picture shows up in the paper, you seem to be with a different woman, while I seldom date."

"Then I'm very pleased you've made an exception for me. As for the number of women I've dated, maybe it's because I haven't found the one I want to spend more time with."

She smiled at him. "Well, good luck in your search."

He couldn't think of anything to say to that. Maybe he'd played up his playboy image a little too much, which would be ironic if he'd turned off the one person he needed to attract.

Jude turned off the highway and followed a winding road back into the hills. When the ground leveled off he pulled into a driveway that opened into a parking lot.

"What a beautiful place," Carina said, looking at what had at one time been a vacation lodge. "The view is awesome." She looked around. "I don't see any signs to tell you this is a restaurant. How does anyone know it's here?"

He took her hand and they walked up the front steps to the wide veranda. "Word of mouth. Reservations are at a premium." He grinned at her. "I'm glad you like it."

She gave his hand a quick squeeze. "I'm pleased that you brought me."

Jude smiled at her obvious pleasure. He still held her hand and she made no effort to pull away. Instead, she stood looking at him with something like wonder and maybe a little bit of trepidation.

"Good evening, Mr. Crenshaw," the maître d' said, as he approached them. "Your table is this way." He escorted them outside onto a large deck overlooking a canyon and rolling hills. The sun was close to the horizon and the few clouds in the sky were already tinted with pink and gold.

Carina sank into her chair, unable to take her eyes from the view. "Oh, Jude," she finally said in a soft voice. "Looking at the sunset makes me feel the same sense of reverence and awe I feel in church. " She looked across the small table at him, her eyes shining.

She was really a beautiful woman. He'd certainly had far worse assignments than spending time with this one.

Their waiter appeared, recited the specials for the night and took their drink orders.

"Does the restaurant have a name?"

"It's listed in the phone book as the Crown Jewel, but

the name doesn't tell a person it's a restaurant. You just have to know what it is and where it is."

Once the sun set behind the hills, twinkle lights lit up the deck and the waiter lit the fat candle on their table for them.

"You picked a good night to be here," the waiter said. "Last night it was too windy to use the deck."

The time flew by for Jude. Carina had a delightful sense of humor, which was usually accompanied by her dazzling smile. He discovered that he really liked her. She was funny and without pretense and he enjoyed her company.

They didn't talk much on the way back to San Antonio. He slipped a CD into the console, one with quiet instrumentals that continued their pleasant mood.

She gave him directions to her apartment building and he found it with no problem. After he opened the front door, he took her hand and didn't release it as they walked up the stairs to the second floor and down the hallway to her apartment. She paused in front of the door and turned to him.

"This has been a magical evening for me," Carina said. "Thank you for inviting me."

"I'm glad to hear it because I'd like to see you again soon." She smiled. "How soon?"

"Tomorrow, and the day after that and the day after that," he said with a grin.

"I'm not sure that's a good idea, is it? Seeing me will slow you down in your hunt for that perfect companion."

He winced. "I'm really not that bad. I'd appreciate it if you'd give me a chance to redeem myself."

Somehow they had moved closer to each other, so close he could lean over and kiss her. Because kissing her seemed so natural, he lowered his head as she raised hers.

He cupped her face in his hands and explored her delectable mouth. She stiffened when he first touched her and he started to pull away and apologize when she relaxed and flowed into his arms.

Jude had no idea how long they stood there. He continued to kiss her and caress her face and shoulders. He knew she could feel the effect she had on him. By the time he finally let her go, he was having trouble breathing and his heart was pumping like an overworked engine.

"I'm sor—" he began. She placed her fingers over his mouth.

"I'm not," she said. "It was a perfect ending for the evening." She stepped back and smiled at him.

He cleared his throat, but still sounded a little hoarse when he said, "You'd better go inside."

Her smile was mischievous. "Yes, that's probably a good idea."

He offered her a rueful look and gave a tiny shrug. "I'll call you tomorrow, okay?" he asked, brushing his knuckles beneath her chin in a soft caress.

She took a deep breath and exhaled, and for a moment she looked a little uncertain. He hadn't realized he'd been holding his breath until she nodded and said, "Okay, I'd like that," and went inside, carefully closing the door between them.

Four

John, Hal and Ruth were in the living room when Jude walked into the house from the garage.

"How was your date?" Ruth asked.

"It's a start. What's going on with y'all?"

John laughed. "Oh, boy. That Texas twang has definitely gotten thicker since we got here, Crenshaw."

Hal said, "I've got a couple of names for you to keep a watch out for—Ross Davies and Patrick Sullivan."

Jude sank into one of the easy chairs. "Who are they?"

"Two of the agents working here who have acquired offshore numbered accounts. They covered their tracks—but not so well that Schilling in Financial couldn't pick them up. And both accounts have very healthy balances."

"Do we know where the deposits came from?"

"No, but we're working on it."

"Interesting."

Ruth spoke up, "After following them for weeks, we finally saw them meeting with Al Patterson."

John said, "If you can get close enough to the family, maybe you'll be able to find out something about them."

"Did you get any information from Carina we don't already have?" Ruth asked.

"Not yet. But I'm working on it."

Hal said, "If you don't impress her, I can always step in for that part of the assignment, Crenshaw."

Jude looked at the cocky agent and made a rude hand gesture, causing the other three to laugh.

"So what's it like to be dating a suspect?" Hal asked more seriously.

"Weird, but this whole setup has been weird. I've gone out with more women in the past six months than I have my entire lifetime."

"Ohh," Ruth said, "Poor baby."

Jude grinned. "Yeah, I know, but when I'm called on to sacrifice myself for the country's security, I'm right there."

Ruth stood and said, "Well, it's getting a little too deep in here for me, so I'll see you guys in the morning." She looked at Hal. "What time do you want to leave?"

"Nine is early enough, I think."

"Well, good night all," Ruth said, and left the room.

Jude looked at John. "Any sign of anyone on the property?"

"Nope. Our cover seems to be working here in the neighborhood."

Jude rolled his eyes. "Hal and Ruth are married, you're her brother and you're all old friends visiting me. Some cover."

"It works," Hal said. "Unfortunately, Ruth isn't interested in playing house once we're inside the house."

"Who are you kidding, Pennington? If Littlefield ever gave you the green light you'd take off running in the opposite direction."

Hal laughed. "True. Very true. I'm not interested in dating any woman who's trained to maim a male in so many ways. I'll keep looking, if it's all the same to everybody."

Jude stretched and yawned. "I'm going to bed now. I've got to figure out a way to see Carina tomorrow and all the days after that."

"Like I say, you've got the toughest assignment of all," Hal pointed out.

Jude would never admit to anyone that he was nervous about getting Carina to go out with him again. Once she had time to think about it, she might decide not to get involved.

Too much was riding on his being the kind of man she might want to date. Any slip could be enough to turn her off.

He thought about his two older brothers and how they would chortle if they knew he was worrying about his sex appeal. He'd always been competitive with them, determined to show them that anything they could do, he could do.

Except get married, of course. He'd leave all that to them.

Jude waited until the next afternoon to call Carina's cell phone. As soon as she answered, he knew she wasn't at home. Background noise said she was at some kind of party. Damn.

"This is Carina."

"Hi. This is Jude. Did I catch you at a bad time?"

"Oh! Hi. I didn't think you really meant it when you said you'd call today."

"If you're busy, I'll call some other time."

She laughed. "Oh, I'm not busy. It's a family tradition that my brothers, their wives and children and I go for

Sunday dinner every week at my parents'. The noise can sometimes reach high decibels before somebody thinks to quiet things down."

"I wondered if you'd like to go for a drive this afternoon. I thought we might head over to Bandera and maybe go to the Lost Maples National Park, stop somewhere on the way back for something to eat. Are you interested?"

When she didn't respond right away, he had a sinking sensation that she was going to say no. He waited.

"I'd like that," she finally said quietly. "I haven't been out in that part of the hills in a long time."

"Me, either, which is why I thought a scenic drive would be nice. When do you want me to pick you up?"

"Oh, in about thirty minutes or so."

"It will take me at least that long to get there from here."

"Where do you live?"

"Just north of town. I'll have to show you the place sometime."

He could have sworn he heard her breath catch. "Maybe sometime," she finally said.

Not that he had any intention of her seeing his living arrangements, but at least he'd gotten a reaction out of her. He wasn't sure what kind, though.

"I'll see you soon." He hung up before she could change her mind.

Carina was outside the house when he pulled up into the driveway. So much for getting to see the rest of the family. Before he had a chance to get out of the car, she opened the passenger door and slid inside. At least she appeared eager to see him, which was encouragement, of sorts.

"Hi," he said, giving her a quick once-over. She wore tan slacks and a sapphire-blue sleeveless top with a scooped neck.

She smiled. "If it seems I'm a little eager to leave, it's because I'm a little eager to leave."

"Ah. I would never have noticed."

She laughed. "I love my family dearly, but sometimes the noise of everybody talking at once and children squealing overwhelms me."

"I'm glad I could play the gallant knight and come rescue you." So much for thinking she might find him irresistible. He supposed his ego could handle the letdown.

She rested her head against the back of her seat. "Sometimes my brothers can be so annoying. They're way too protective of me."

"They didn't like you coming out with me this afternoon?"

"Al didn't say that. What he did was ask where we were going and when I expected to get back, as though I were sixteen."

"I hope that you convinced him that I'm perfectly harmless."

Carina sputtered into laughter. "No one meeting you could ever be convinced that you're harmless, Jude. I think he and the rest of the family are curious, that's all. As I told you last night, I haven't dated in a while. My brothers would probably prefer that I become a nun!"

"I feel doubly honored that you agreed to see me, if that's the case."

"I enjoyed being with you last night. Plus, I suppose I was curious, too."

"Oh. Then it wasn't my charm and sparkling personality that wowed you? I'm crushed."

"With your reputation, I figured I'd be safe enough, knowing you'd be moving on after a few dates."

"You make me sound like a heartless jerk."

"No. It's just that since you're a very handsome man,

come from a highly respected family, don't need to work for a living and you're single, I'm sure many women are eager to spend time with you."

"You have a positive knack for making what some could consider a compliment sound like an indictment of my character." He looked over at her. "Are you going to tell me you don't want to see me again? Because if you are, I sincerely hope you'll allow me to make a case for myself first."

"There's no need. I enjoy your company and don't mind seeing you. I have no fear of getting too involved with you before you get bored with me."

"Ouch. You really know how to hurt a guy. You must have had some really bad dating experiences to form your opinion about men. Or is it just me?"

She didn't answer right away and he decided he'd better stay quiet.

Finally, she said, "I was engaged once." She glanced at him from the corner of her eye before continuing. "We met in high school, became friends, and later dated. Danny was my best friend. We enjoyed each other's company and when I returned home from New York after Dad's stroke, it seemed only natural to become engaged. I don't know what I would have done during that time without Danny being there for me. The family was pleased to see me happy and ready to settle down. We talked about my desire to get my music degree from Juilliard and Danny told me he was willing to move to New York while I attended school, whenever I was ready to return."

He turned into a scenic pull-off and stopped the car. After he unfastened his seat belt, he turned to face her and asked, "What happened, Carina?"

She looked away as though taking in the view. "My life

fell apart," she said quietly. "While I was spending my days with Mom and Dad and taking Dad to physical therapy, I always made certain I was home in the evenings. Dan worked for the company. He made a run once a week to the Rio Grande Valley. The company has a warehouse there. Late one night Al called to say that Danny had been killed in an auto accident on his way back to San Antonio. I was devastated. As if that wasn't enough, I learned a few weeks later that he'd had a woman with him at the time."

Jude looked at her in surprise. He'd read the accident report and there was no mention of a woman having been involved. He'd seen the photographs, as well. No one could have walked away from the mangled mess that had been a car.

"Ah, Carina," he said, touching her shoulder. "I'm so sorry. Almost losing your father and then losing your fiancé must have been really tough." She sat with her clenched hands in her lap. "Did you find out who the woman was?"

She shook her head. "No. I happened to overhear a conversation between Alfredo and Benito. They were talking about Danny and the woman he'd been seeing in Weslaco and how shocked and disappointed they were when they found out about her. I confronted them and demanded to know the truth. They reluctantly told me about the woman."

He'd have to check the accident report again because he was positive there'd been no one else in the car. If that were true, why would her brothers lie, knowing the added pain they were causing her?

Jude took one of her hands and uncurled her fingers, placing them in his outstretched hand. He stroked her fingers and could feel the tremor in her body that she was trying so hard to hide.

"I felt so stupid," she said, as though to herself. "And so blind. How could I not have known he was seeing someone else? I'd trusted him completely. I'd loved him, believed in him and then I find out after he's dead that he had betrayed everything we had together."

They sat there quietly until Carina roused herself from her memories. "Guaranteed downer on a date," she said, forcing a smile. "Talking about our former loves. Sorry about that. If you have any exes you'd like to talk about, I'll be happy to listen." When she realized what she'd said, she blushed. "Or maybe not. We don't have that kind of time, do we?"

He grabbed his chest. "I didn't see that one coming! Truth is, Carina, I've never been seriously involved with any woman." He lifted his shoulder and added, "I guess that says it all, doesn't it? But I don't go around deliberately hurting people, either. The women I've dated know going in that I'm not looking for anything serious."

"Like us."

He nodded. "Like us."

Jude's conscience nudged him. He had to make certain that he kept their relationship casual, that he made it clear to Carina that he saw her as a friend. He'd have to be very careful or she would end up feeling betrayed again when this assignment was over.

He very deliberately lightened the mood for the rest of the afternoon. They got out and walked at various places, looked for fossils among the rocks and ate at a small café in Uvalde while Jude regaled her with tales of his childhood and what chaos four young boys could cause.

By the time he took her home that evening, she seemed lighthearted and relaxed. Her eyes sparkled and he had a tough time keeping his distance from her.

He walked her to her door as he had the night before. "Thank you for coming with me this afternoon. You made it much more enjoyable than if I'd gone alone," he said.

"And I'm willing to admit that, just maybe, your reputation has been somewhat exaggerated and you're really a nice guy."

He picked her up in his arms and swung her around in a circle, laughing with unfettered amusement. When he realized what he'd done, he hastily placed her back on her feet and stepped away. "I, uh, didn't mean to do that. I know you want to keep this casual and I honor your feelings." He put his hand out as though to shake hers. "Guess I'd better get out of here before I ruin your new opinion of me."

She looked at his hand and laughed. "We're shaking hands now I take it?"

He could feel his ears burning. "Yeah. No more kissing. That could get me into some real trouble."

The look she gave him was mysterious and beguiling. She dropped her lashes before looking up again. "Don't worry, Jude, your virtue is safe with me."

Five

The following Friday evening, Jude stood in front of his bathroom mirror grumbling to himself. He hated ties. They were the work of the devil, he was certain. He'd tied the one he'd chosen three times and it refused to hang straight.

"Aw, to hell with it," he said, glaring at his image.

He had on the dark gray pants to one of his suits and a white dress shirt because, once again, he was taking Carina out.

He'd seen her twice this week, and she appeared to enjoy his company. Regardless of the teasing he got from the other agents, Jude was on edge whenever he was with her.

She was a good-looking woman and he was a red-blooded male…so of course he wanted to take her to bed and get her out of his system. That wasn't going to happen, although he'd gotten the impression from a couple of subtle comments she'd made that she wouldn't be averse to the idea.

Sleeping with a suspect wasn't part of his job description. He wouldn't normally have a problem with the idea, except for the fact that his body went on full alert whenever he was around her. It was downright embarrassing.

Since Sunday evening when she'd made fun of him for not kissing her good-night, he'd made certain that, after each date when he walked her to the door of her apartment, he'd kissed her. Each kiss was more intense than the last one and by the time he'd left her last night, he was trembling with desire. The cold shower hadn't helped much. Nor had his dream about going inside her apartment with her in his arms, finding her bed and making passionate love to her all night.

So Jude was in a lousy mood this evening and his recalcitrant tie hadn't helped a whole hell of a lot.

He grabbed his suit jacket off the back of a chair and was headed toward the bedroom door when his phone rang.

He walked back and picked up the phone beside his bed. "Crenshaw."

He heard a familiar male laughter. "Hey, bro, just thought I'd let you know that there's yet another Crenshaw male in the world now. He was born a couple of hours ago, weighed in at a little over eight pounds and has a healthy pair of lungs."

Jude sat on the side of the bed and smiled for the first time that day. "Congratulations, Jake. That's great news. How's Ashley doing?"

"She's exhausted, but she's fine. She said she'd have much more sympathy the next time she helped to deliver a foal or a calf." Ashley Crenshaw was a veterinarian and had offices in New Eden.

"Have you named him yet?"

"Nope. We can't seem to agree on his name. Ashley wants to name him after her dad, Ken. I want to continue the tradition of using a name starting with J. Now that he's here, we'll have to come to some kind of agreement."

"Maybe this is much too simple, but why not give him two names?"

"She might go along with that, but she doesn't want to stick him with the name Jeremiah."

"Ah. So you think he should be named after the founder of our family dynasty, I take it."

"We could call him Jerry, but she doesn't like it."

"Well, I'm sure you'll work it out before long. Of course you could always call him B.B. Crenshaw."

"Meaning what?"

"Baby Boy Crenshaw. Once he's walking you can drop the Baby part of his name and call him Boy. Maybe by the time he graduates from high school you two strong-minded people will have agreed on a name you both like or he can pick a name for himself."

"You know, Jude, you're not being much help."

Jude laughed. "I have faith that the two of you will am-icably work out the matter."

"So when are you coming up to meet your brand-new nephew? Heather's eager to show him off and Dad wants to throw a barbecue."

"Of course he does. Dad wants to have a barbecue ev-ery time the mail's delivered. So Heather isn't upset about having a little brother?"

"Not yet. Of course that might change once we get him home and the reality of not being the only child finally hits her. She'll be going to kindergarten this fall, and we're hop-ing that will make her feel all grown up, since she can do so many things her brother can't." Jake paused. "You didn't answer my question, you know. When are you coming home to visit?"

Jude sighed. "Good question. The assignment is moving into its final phase and I don't know how much time I can spare. I'll get up there to meet my nephew as soon as I can."

"The folks miss you."

"I know. I miss them. Once this assignment is over, I promise to take a real vacation and come stay with you and Ashley for several days. It's an uncle's prerogative to spoil Heather and Baby Boy."

"Get here when you can. I know you can't talk about your assignment, but be careful, okay?"

"Always. Thanks for calling, Jake. Tell Ashley I'm very proud of her and to stick to her guns. If she wants that baby named after Ken, she should have her way."

"Oh, great. So you want me to tell her my own brother supports her on this name thing!"

Jude smiled. "Yeah, I do. I'll call when it looks as though I can get away from here." He replaced the receiver and stood, still smiling.

When he went downstairs he saw that John, Hal and Ruth were watching a cable movie in the den. He wished he could join them. In fact, he'd be more eager to face a root canal than the date tonight.

Ruth glanced up and saw him. "My, oh, my. Don't we look fine. So where are you going tonight, lover boy?"

The other two looked at him and waited for his answer.

There was no help for it. "We have tickets to see a ballet." He mumbled the last word.

"A ballet?" Hal repeated, laughing. "The fun never stops for you, does it, pal?"

"Ballets are beautiful," Ruth said, frowning at Hal. "I wish I could go."

"Believe me, I wish you could go instead of me," Jude replied.

Wouldn't Jake have hooted if he'd known Jude's plans for the evening? He would never let him live it down if the truth came out.

"See ya later," he said to the trio and went to the garage where his baby waited.

One bright spot in this assignment was being able to use his car. He'd found a certain satisfaction watching her climb the winding hills like a mountain goat whenever he left town and headed for the Hill Country. He enjoyed putting her through her paces.

After he tapped on Carina's door, he happened to glance at his watch and saw that he was a little early. Traffic had been lighter than he'd expected and he'd caught most of the lights green on the way to her place.

When she opened the door, she was wearing a soft, shimmering robe that lovingly hugged her curves and he almost groaned out loud.

"I'm sorry," he said before she had a chance to speak. "I didn't realize how early I was until after I tapped on the door. You want me to drive around the block a few times?"

She laughed and took his hand, pulling him into the apartment. "Don't be silly. Have a seat and I'll be ready in a few minutes."

A whiff of her perfume wafted around him, causing his muscles to contract. He deliberately turned away and sat in one of her chairs. "Take your time," he said. "There's no rush."

Once he was alone, Jude looked around her apartment. Hal had already been through it this week while she was with Jude. He hadn't found anything incriminating. In fact, he had found nothing relating to the family business at all.

So now what? Maybe Carina wasn't part of the smuggling operation but at this point he had no way of knowing. As far as he was concerned, being a Patterson was reason enough to suspect her.

When she returned, Carina wore an elegant black dress and stiletto heels. Tonight she wore her hair loose around her shoulders. Being totally objective, Jude decided that she looked stunning.

He stood and said, "Ready?"

She picked up a small purse lying on a table nearby. "Yes, I am. Thank you for your patience."

"No problem."

Once outside her apartment he took the keys from her hand and locked the door. "You need a security system," he said, thinking of Hal's visit. There wasn't a lock made that couldn't be disengaged by a pro. The idea was to make it as difficult as possible in order to discourage any would-be burglar.

Once in the car, Carina said, "You seem unusually quiet tonight. Is there something wrong?"

Pulled out of his reverie, he quickly said, "Oh! Nothing's wrong." If you didn't count the fact that he would soon be sitting for a couple of hours watching people prancing around on their tiptoes. "As a matter of fact, I received some good news just before I left. My brother Jake called to say his son was born this afternoon."

"Oh, that's great news. Jake's your oldest brother, right?"

"Right."

"And his wife's name is— I'm sorry, I forget."

"Ashley. She was raised on the ranch with us. Since she's two years younger than me, I've known her all her life. She and Jake make a great team."

"Oh! Speaking of family. Al is having a cookout at his place tomorrow afternoon and I was wondering if you'd like to come with me."

A jolt of adrenaline shot through him. Yes! This was what he'd been waiting for.

"Sure. Sounds fun. What time?"

"Around two or so. We probably won't eat until five or thereabout. Be sure to bring a swimsuit. He and Marisa have a huge swimming pool tucked away behind sturdy fencing, so the children can't go near it without an adult."

He made a mental note to buy a swimsuit tomorrow. He figured cut-off jeans wouldn't do for a Patterson family gathering.

They arrived at the theatre a few minutes before the opening act. Once seated, Jude unobtrusively adjusted his legs in an attempt to find adequate legroom.

Carina leaned over to him and asked, "Have you seen this ballet before?"

He gave her a straight look. "Guess it's confession time. The truth is that I've never seen *any* ballet before."

Her eyes widened. "Really?" she asked, looking more amused than the comment warranted.

"'Fraid not."

"Then why did you ask me to go to this one?"

"Because you mentioned earlier in the week that the touring group would be here this weekend, so I figured you might want to see it."

She kissed him on the cheek and said, "You are full of surprises, Mr. Crenshaw."

He could feel his face heating up. "Yeah, well…" What could he say? I have orders to spend as much time with you as I can? I'm actually getting paid for this? Somehow, he didn't figure she'd be pleased to hear the truth.

The orchestra started the overture and they fell silent.

It was sometime during the last act that Carina nudged

him. He opened his eyes, realizing that he'd fallen asleep. She leaned over and whispered in his ear. "I don't mind your sleeping through the performance but your snoring is disturbing others!"

He quickly glanced around him with an apologetic look. A man behind him grinned and whispered, "My sentiments exactly," which earned him an elbow in his ribs from his wife.

When the thing was finally over—had it really lasted the entire weekend or did it just seem that way?—he stood with the rest of the audience and clapped politely. Actually, he was so glad to have it over that he clapped with great sincerity.

Carina waited until they left the building and were on the way to the car before she said, "I take it you don't care much for ballet."

He glanced at her and saw her face filled with mirth. "I'm truly sorry for embarrassing you this evening. I must have been more tired than I thought."

"How do you feel about opera?"

"Opera?" he repeated, attempting to hide his horror. "Uh, well, I'm not sure…"

"Because you've never been to an opera, either, right?"

"I confess, ma'am. You've got me dead to rights."

She broke into infectious laughter and he finally joined her. Once in the car she said, "Tell me this. If you could do anything you want tonight, what would it be? And I want an honest answer."

He turned in his seat and looked at her. The light from the street lamp made her fair skin glow in the shadows. "Honestly?" He thought about it for a minute or two and then said, "I would probably be at a country-and-western bar that had live music."

"Sounds good. Let's do that."

He studied her searchingly. She wasn't the bar-scene type, unless it was a coffee bar. "You sure?"

"Absolutely. And if I start snoring, you can poke me."

He laughed. "Oh, I don't think you'll fall asleep."

He pulled out of the parking lot and drove to the Crazy Eights roadhouse. They could hear the music blasting from a half block away. By the time they parked, Carina was the one laughing, "Do they offer earplugs?" she asked, when he opened her door for her.

Jude grinned and shook his head. "We don't have to go inside, you know."

She stood and straightened her spine. "Of course we do. You did something tonight you've never done before. Now it's my turn."

He couldn't help but chuckle. Carina was a pistol, sure enough. She was every inch a lady as she stood there looking at him with strong determination.

"Well, if we're going in there, I'm going to get rid of this—" he yanked off his tie "—and this…" His coat came off next. He tossed both of them into the car, "and roll up my sleeves," which he proceeded to do. He opened the top two buttons on his shirt, let out a sigh of satisfaction and held out his hand. "C'mon, tiger, you're about to have an experience you'll never forget!"

Jude had to admit the band had overdone it a little with the volume on the amps. Of course the place was huge, with a dance floor big enough to accommodate a slew of dancers moving in a comfortable circle as they did various dances. The place was packed, so maybe the band wanted to make sure they were heard.

He glanced at Carina, who was looking around her as though she'd been dropped onto another planet. He stepped ahead of her, still grasping her hand, while he wove a path in and around people and tables until he saw a waitress clearing off several glasses and beer bottles from a tall table with high seats. He casually lifted Carina onto one of them.

"Now that wasn't necessary," she said, laughing. "I'm not that short!"

"Just thought I'd save you some time."

"What can I get you?" the waitress asked, holding a full tray of empties.

Jude glanced at Carina and raised his brows. "Uh, whatever you're having," she said in response.

Trying to hide his amusement, he ordered two bottles of beer and the waitress left.

"Have you ever had beer before?"

"No. But this is my night for firsts, right?"

"Looks like it."

He made a point not to react when she made a slight face at her first taste of her drink once it arrived. After that, she carefully sipped while she watched the dancers.

"Wanna dance?" he asked after ten minutes or so.

She glanced at her shoes. "I'm not sure I can. Those are some fairly vigorous dances they're doing."

"I'll be gentle. I won't swing you around like that guy just did. He and his partner have been dancing together long enough to know each other's moves."

She took a large swallow of beer, tried not to choke and nodded to him. "Okay. I'll try it," she said, sounding a little hoarse.

Her feet were several inches off the floor, sitting there. "May I?" he asked, placing his hands at her waist. She nodded and he picked her up and placed her on the floor.

Once on the dance floor he stayed on the edges and showed her the steps. She quickly learned them and her natural sense of rhythm took over. Before long, they were out there dancing with the best of them.

When the band finally took a break, they were warm and breathless. As soon as they sat down, she finished off her glass of rather stale beer. He signaled for two more and when they arrived, she drank almost half of hers without stopping. "Whew!" she said, waving her hands at her face. "That was quite a workout!"

"You did just fine out there."

She grinned with delight. "I did, didn't I? The steps aren't hard and it's fun to sail around the room like that."

He poured the rest of her beer into her glass. "How's the beer?"

"Oh! Well, actually it tastes good after all that exercise." She drank some more. "I didn't think I was going to like it at first, but it grows on you, doesn't it?"

He nodded solemnly. "It certainly does that." He looked around and saw that several couples were leaving. "Are you ready to go?"

She looked shocked by the idea. "Oh, no! Isn't the band going to play some more?"

"Yeah, they have another set."

"Then if it's okay with you, I'd like to stay."

"Good enough."

They closed the roadhouse down. Since she'd been drinking beer as though it was water, Carina was a little unsteady on her feet by the time they left. He managed to get her into the car, fastened her seat belt and went around to the driver's side. Once he was in the car, Carina said, "Jude?"

"Mmm?"

He started the car and backed out of the parking space.

"Tell me something." She carefully enunciated each word.

"If I can."

They drove through empty streets for several minutes before she asked, "Can you get drunk on beer?"

He bit the inside of his cheek, determined not to show his amusement. "What do you think?"

"I'm not sure. I drink wine once in a while but I never felt quite like this before."

"Don't worry about it. I'll get you home and you can sleep it off."

"Jude."

"Yes?"

"I didn't fall asleep tonight."

"No, ma'am, you certainly didn't."

"Nobody could sleep with all that noise going on."

"True."

"I've gotta admit going dancing was more fun than the ballet, although the ballet was good, too."

"I'm glad you enjoyed your evening."

Silence.

"Jude."

"Yes, Carina?"

"I like you."

"Thank you. I like you, too."

"You're fun to be with."

"Right back at you."

"And you're a good dancer."

"Thank you, again."

"And…there was a bunch of women watching you, did you know that?"

"No, I didn't know that."

She smiled blissfully. "I didn't think so. You don't have a roving eye."

"Uh…thank you. I think."

"I'm so sleepy now that it's quiet. Maybe I'll go to sleep after all."

"No need," he said, pulling into a parking space next to her apartment building. "We're here." He took her purse from her limp hand and removed the key and then he walked around to her side of the car. She didn't say a word when he picked her up and carried her inside the building.

He put her on her feet in front of her door and unlocked it, then guided her into the apartment and on into her bedroom. "Now you can sleep," he said softly.

She turned and looked at him. "You can stay if you'd like."

"Uh, that's very sweet of you, but I need to get home and you need to get some rest."

She turned her back and asked, "Would you unzip me, please?"

He sincerely wished that her slightly inebriated state was a complete turnoff to him. Unfortunately, he found her loose-limbed demeanor adorable, but oh, was she going to hate herself in the morning.

He unzipped the dress and she dropped her arms so that the sleeves slid down her arms and the dress continued falling to the floor, leaving her in a wisp of a bra and panties, her hose and heels.

He closed his eyes and tried not to groan. She turned around and looked at him and his mouth went dry. "Well." He cleared his throat. "I'll see you tomorrow." He took a step back from her.

She followed him.

"Aren't you going to kiss me good-night?"

This was *so* not funny. He wasn't used to showing restraint around a practically nude young woman. In his experience, by the time they reached this stage, both parties knew they would end up in bed together.

He leaned down and gave her a quick kiss, at least it would have been quick if she hadn't pulled his head closer and wrapped her arms around his neck. Her body trembled. Or maybe that was his. Either way, he had to get out of here and fast!

He unfastened her arms and said, "Good night, Carina," hightailing it out the door as if a posse was after him.

All the way home and long into the night, Jude relived those moments in her bedroom. Worse than that, his body refused to forgive him for turning down her invitation to spend the night.

He should be used to living in a constant state of arousal by now, because from all indications, being aroused was going to be a permanent condition as long as he was working this case.

An annoying ringing in her ear woke Carina the next morning, and she hit her alarm to stop the jangling noise. Only it wouldn't stop. She opened one eye and saw it was ten-fifteen and realized the noise came from the phone. She picked it up and pushed the Talk button. "H'lo."

"Aha! Still in bed, are you?" Marisa said. "Are you alone?"

"Yes."

"You sound terrible."

"Good. Because I feel worse."

"Are you coming down with the flu?"

"I have a hunch that what I'm battling is the granddaddy of all hangovers."

"Hangovers! Are you saying you got drunk at the ballet last night?"

Carina groaned. "Please don't shout and no, I didn't get drunk at the ballet last night. I seem to have had a wee bit too much to drink at Crazy Eights last night."

There was silence on the phone. Then Marisa said, "Go take some aspirin, try to eat something and then call me back because I want to know how an evening at the ballet ended up at some place with such an outlandish name."

Carina nodded and hung up the phone. "Oh. 'Bye," she mumbled to the receiver, only then realizing she'd hung up on her friend.

Whatever.

She gingerly got out of bed and went to take a shower. She saw herself in the mirror and realized that she'd slept in her underwear. What was that all about?

While she stood beneath the soothing spray of water, Carina recalled the night before. By the time she finished with her shower, she was smiling at her memories.

Jude had been a perfect gentleman. He'd also been a great deal of fun to be with. She loved the dances she'd learned as they moved with the crowd around the dance floor and she hoped they would go there again sometime. Maybe next time she'd just drink water, though.

By the time she dressed and went into the kitchen for some much-needed coffee, Carina decided that beer wouldn't be on her preferred list of alcoholic drinks ever again.

Once she'd nibbled on a piece of toast and had three large cups of coffee, Carina called Marisa back.

"Well?" Marisa answered.

Caller ID was a wonderful thing.

"After the ballet—where Jude fell asleep, by the way— we went to a country-and-western place and danced until one in the morning. Muscles I didn't know I had are complaining but I had a terrific time."

"How's your head?"

"Better."

"This doesn't sound at all like you, Carina. The ballet,

yes. And he actually fell asleep? Oh, that's funny. But a country-and-western bar?"

"With live music. I know. Since he was obviously bored with the ballet, I wanted to see what he liked to do, and you know something, Marisa, I can't remember ever having so much fun. I loved it!"

"So you're going to learn how to play country music, are you?"

"Uh…no. But I don't mind dancing to it."

"So. Did he stay once he took you home?"

"No, he didn't."

"How do you feel about that?"

"I'm okay with it. Although I think I'm ready to move the relationship up a notch or two. There's no doubt in my mind he'd be a wonderful lover. Maybe he's just waiting for me to give him some kind of signal. Wish I knew what it was."

"Is he coming this afternoon?"

"Yes. Or at least he said he would last night."

"Wear your bikini."

Carina laughed. "Good idea."

"I'll see you later."

Six

Carina was French-braiding her hair that same morning when the phone rang. She looked at her hair, looked at the phone, shrugged and released her hair, which immediately unwound itself.

"Hello."

"Good morning. How are you feeling this morning?"

She cleared her throat. "Better, thank you. Did I make a complete fool of myself last night?"

"Not at all. You seemed to be enjoying yourself."

"Oh, I was. From now on, though, I believe I'll lay off the beer."

Jude laughed. "Whatever you say. I called to see when I should pick you up?"

She looked at the clock. It was almost one o'clock. "Around two will be fine. People will begin to trickle into the party as the afternoon progresses. In the meantime, it will be mostly family. It will give you a chance to get to know my family a little better."

He didn't answer right away. "Yeah, that would be nice. I'd like to find out how your family survived you growing up. I'm surprised they're not either white-haired or bald."

"I'll have you know I was a perfect little lady growing up."

"Uh-huh. Don't forget, I've seen your wild streak. You can't hide it any longer."

"Oh, by the way, why don't we get season tickets for the ballet since you enjoy sleeping to the music?"

"Blackmail, is it? I don't mention your wild side and you don't mention ballet."

"You got it."

"Well, I'll see you around two," he said.

Jude hung up the phone and went downstairs.

"What's on your agenda today?" Hal asked. "Other than continuing to see a sexy woman."

"She may be sexy," Jude replied, "but she's still a suspect, don't forget."

John spoke up. "We don't forget that, but the way you bring it up in every conversation makes me wonder if you need to be reminded."

"Nope. As a matter of fact, we're going to her brother Al's house for a cookout this afternoon. She thinks I should get better acquainted with the family."

"Way to go, man," John said. "You're definitely getting in with the kin."

Ruth looked at him thoughtfully. "It sounds as though she might be getting serious about you. Is that a possibility?"

Jude laughed. "I hardly think so. She's made it clear that she's seeing me in order to get back into a social life. I have to watch that I keep her booked up enough for her not to spend time with other people. I'm ready to end this case.

Remember, I was on vacation when this assignment came up and I really am ready for one."

Ruth smiled. "Well, keep up the good work and we'll all be back home soon."

Alfred Patterson lived in a gated community that looked to be new, if the signs of continued construction in the area were any indication. When Jude and Carina stopped at the gate, a security guard took down the license number of his car and gave them a visitor's card to place on the dash.

Jude had made a point when he first came back to Texas of changing his Maryland plates. He'd given the ranch as his home address. Anyone deciding to check him out would see that he was just who he said he was.

As they drove past the gates, Jude asked, "How long has your brother lived here?"

"I think it's been about a year now. The business has been doing so well that he wanted a larger place where he could do more entertaining, like today."

He followed her directions and when he saw the house it was obvious that the business was doing quite well. They parked along the wide driveway and walked around to the back, where the sounds of squeals and splashing intermingled with laughter and conversations.

There were almost a dozen people there and Jude immediately recognized two of them from the photos he'd been shown: Ross Davies and Patrick Sullivan were standing by the outdoor grill talking to Al.

"I'll introduce you to the people I know," Carina said, "and let Al do the rest."

He noticed that Ben's wife was pregnant. She sat in the shade with Marisa. When Marisa saw them she jumped up and hurried toward them. "There you are. Just in time to get something to drink and find a cool spot in the shade."

Jude saw that besides the large swimming pool, there was a tennis court, as well. The lawn was as smooth as a putting green with large trees and flowerbeds arranged artistically.

"You have a beautiful home," he said to Marisa.

Marisa smiled. "Well, let's say it's considerably larger than what we had. I ended up hiring help for the house and the lawn." She laughed. "I'm not complaining, you understand, but it took a little while to get used to it." She looked over at Al and said, "C'mon. I'll have Al introduce you to some of our neighbors."

"Oh?"

"I believe their wives are related or something. You rarely see one without the other." She stopped beside Al. "Jude Crenshaw is here, Alfredo."

Carina's brother turned and looked at him. "Glad you could make it," he said, politely. He held out his hand and Jude shook it.

"And these are a couple of our friends," Marisa went on to say.

Al took over the introductions. "Ross Davies, Patrick Sullivan, meet Mr. Crenshaw."

Ross was short and a little overweight. Patrick looked like he was barely out of college. He was tall and trim.

"Gentlemen," Jude said, and shook hands briefly.

"Crenshaw," Ross said. "That name sounds familiar."

"There's a lot of us in the state."

"Ah. Maybe that's where I heard the name. What do you do, Jude?"

Jude laughed. "As little as possible. How about you?"

"I'm between jobs at the moment, thinking about taking early retirement."

Jude nodded. "Sounds like a plan."

"Old Pat here," Ross continued, "he's a gung-ho government-worker type. Pushes papers, fills out forms, all that good stuff."

"Doesn't sound like much fun to me," Jude replied with a smile.

Sullivan said, "Maybe not, but it pays the bills."

The two men and Al laughed as though he'd said something funny.

Marisa spoke up. "Are your wives coming?"

Ross said, "Mary Ann said she hoped to make it, but wasn't sure. Our oldest is running a fever and she doesn't want to leave him with the nanny unless his fever goes down."

Pat said, "My wife will be here a little later. She had errands to run and wasn't certain when she'd be back."

"Help yourself to something cold to drink, Jude," Al said. "If you feel like playing a game of tennis, Patrick, here, is your man. He played on his varsity team when he was at college. Plus we have the pool when you're ready to cool off."

"They didn't teach much tennis where I come from," Jude said with a drawl. "All us kids were too busy working on the family ranch."

He noted the brief eye contact between the agents. They'd pegged him as a lightweight.

Carina, who had been quietly standing beside Jude, said, "We'll see you later," to Al and the two men. "I'm ready to find a comfortable, shady spot and become a sloth."

Later that afternoon, several of them went swimming and Jude saw Carina in a swimsuit that left little to the imagination. Carina's underwear the night before had at least three times the material.

"Are you going to swim in that?" he said, raising his brows. If any part of it shrunk at all, she would be nude.

She looked up at him and smiled. "More like dog paddle. But don't mind me. Do all the swimming you want."

Jude swam several laps before he got his unruly body calmed down. How much was a man supposed to take, anyway? The more he was around her, the more he wanted to make love to her. Lust had a power all its own. The trick was to ignore it, which he was doing.

Yeah, right.

When most of the guests had left and while Carina was inside putting away the remains of the party with her sisters-in-law, Al sat down beside him at one of the tables on the stone terrace.

He leaned forward and said quietly, "I'd like to talk to you about Carina for a moment."

"She's really something, isn't she? You must be very proud of her."

"You've been giving her the rush, I understand."

"That's right." Jude met Al's gaze without flinching. "You have a problem with that?"

"I don't want to see her hurt. She's gone through a lot of bad stuff and she's vulnerable at the moment."

"Do you think I'm going to hurt her?"

"You have quite a reputation with the ladies, Crenshaw."

Jude laughed. "As do you, my friend," he replied, lifting his glass of beer to him.

Al looked startled. "Not since I married Marisa," he finally said.

Oh, no. You're much more discreet now. "You see? A man can change when he decides to settle down, don't you agree?" Since Al hadn't changed much, Jude looked forward to hearing him explain his double standard.

"Are you saying you're ready to settle down?"

"It's way too early in our relationship to tell, but you get my point. If people in general have a good enough reason, they'll change." He paused for a moment and then said softly, "Are you asking if my intentions are honorable?"

Al flushed and glanced over his shoulder at the house. "Of course not! Carina doesn't like me meddling in her affairs."

"Do you do that often?" Jude asked with a half smile.

"Did she tell you she was once engaged?"

"She mentioned it."

"She was much too good for him, but she couldn't see it. I mean, he had no ambition, not much money and so I gave him a job doing mostly gofer work. I knew they were friends and all but when she told me they were planning to get married, I couldn't believe it!"

"Carina mentioned he was killed in an auto accident."

Al made a face. "Yeah."

"I've been curious, but didn't want to ask her about the details. Was she with him at the time?"

"No, thank God. He'd been down in south Texas at a warehouse we have there and was returning home. It was quite late, almost two o'clock in the morning, the police said. They said he was speeding, lost control of the car and rolled it, killing him."

"Losing him must have been really tough for her. I guess that's why when I first met her she told me she didn't go out much."

"Well, you seem to have made up for that lack during the past week!"

Jude laughed. "That's true." He leaned back in his chair and asked, "What, exactly, do you do in a business like yours? I mean, what do you import and export?"

Jude waited to see if Al would allow the change of subject. Al looked as though he wanted to say something more about Jude's relationship with Carina. When he looked at the house again he saw the three women coming toward him. As though they'd been discussing the business the entire time, Al said, "We buy and sell all kinds of things—antique furniture from Europe, specialty items from the Middle East and Asia. Ben does most of the buying while I do the day-to-day work here. Dad is a fine man, a wonderful husband and a caring father, but he was a deplorable businessman. By the time he had the stroke—in fact, I believe worrying about the business brought on the stroke—he was close to being forced into bankruptcy. Since Ben and I took over, we've rebuilt the business, modernized it, made new contacts overseas, started buying some lower-end and more marketable items. We've managed to turn things around."

"I'm impressed."

Carina walked up behind Jude and put her hands on his shoulders, kneading them. "You're impressed about what?" she asked.

He glanced around and she smiled at him. "All you industrious types, working hard every day. It makes me weary just to hear what it takes to run a business."

Al gave him a condescending smile. "Guess you don't have to work with the money the Crenshaws earn off their various enterprises."

Jude stood and stretched. "I can't complain." He dropped his arm around Carina's shoulders. "You 'bout ready to go, tiger?"

They took their leave from her family. As soon as they got into the car, Carina asked, "What were you and Al really talking about all huddled together this evening?"

"He was telling me about the business."

"Before that."

"Ah. He was warning me not to hurt you."

She groaned. "Of course he was. Why he's appointed himself my guardian I will never know. He knows how much I hate it when he gets involved in my personal life."

"Yeah, he did mention something like that."

"Not that it stopped him."

"Hey, he's just looking after his sister. If I had a sister, I'd probably be the same way with her, vetting all her dates, that sort of thing."

"Perhaps...if she were sixteen and still in high school. How does he think I managed to live in New York for three years?"

"Sowed a little wild oats, did we?"

She laughed. "Actually, I didn't. I spent my time practicing and attending classes. Besides, Danny was a big part of my life."

They pulled up in front of her apartment building and got out of the car.

On the way upstairs Jude said lightly, "I'm glad you're willing to go out with me."

"I've enjoyed being with you," she replied.

Once her door was open, Carina said, "It's still early, if you'd like to come in for a while."

He brushed his finger beneath her chin. "I can't," he said ruefully. He kissed her and quickly stepped away. "I'll call you," he said, wishing for the moment that this assignment was over and that she'd been cleared. The truth was that he did enjoy her.

Of course he wouldn't become seriously involved with her. He liked his freedom too much for that. Besides, neither of them were looking for anything other than a few laughs and some fun times.

* * *

Ruth and Hal were waiting for him in the living room when he got home.

"What's up, guys?" Jude asked, relaxing into one of the comfortable chairs.

Hal answered. "The bug in their office worked. Al and Ben are going to Mexico City next Thursday on a buying trip. Think we should go?"

"Definitely. Since they haven't seen you, the two of you could blend in as tourists seeing the sights. If they spotted me, they could get suspicious. Which reminds me. According to Al Patterson, Carina's fiancé was going too fast, lost control and flipped over. No mention of his having been sideswiped."

"Maybe they don't know that part," Ruth suggested.

"Or maybe they caused that part," Jude replied.

"We also picked up another interesting conversation Al had with one of his relatives in Mexico City. It appears that neither his parents nor his sister know anything about what he and his brother have been doing and he made it clear to his cousin or uncle that they weren't to find out. The 'or else' hung silently in his tone."

Jude felt a moment of strong relief and justified the feeling to himself. Carina and her parents were nice people. They didn't deserve to be brought up on charges because of the brothers' illegal activity.

His relief had nothing to do with the fact that he was no longer dating one of the suspects. Of course he needed to continue to see her to stay close to her brothers despite the struggle he was having with his libido.

John came wandering out of the den and asked Jude, "Did you get any interesting information for us today?"

"I got to meet Davies and Sullivan. The three of them seem real buddy-buddy."

"It's certainly enough to cause suspicions to be raised, even though they could say they're trying to get information on the family," John said.

"Have you found out who deposited the money in their offshore accounts?" Jude asked.

"I've found out that they've done some very sophisticated work hiding the source. I'm still working on it. I've traced the money out of the country but haven't been able to locate where it came from."

"Geez," Hal said. "You've been working on this for months. It can't be all that difficult, can it?"

"Why, no, Hal, of course not. Why don't you finish it up for me?"

Jude and Ruth laughed. Ruth said, "Now, now, boys, play nicely or we'll take away your toys and make you go home."

"I wish!" Hal snorted. "Okay. So Ruth and I will play tourists in Mexico City this week. John will continue the very intricate tracing of the money Davies and Sullivan are now enjoying and then there's you, Jude. Got any plans?"

"I'm fairly certain I won't be attending any more ballets any time soon," he mused.

Seven

"**W**ell?" Marisa said as soon as Carina picked up the phone the next morning.

"Good morning to you, too, Marisa."

"Did he stay over last night?"

"You show more interest in my sex life than your own."

"Listen, honey, you have a better chance of *having* a sex life than I do. You wouldn't believe some of the excuses I keep getting for why he doesn't come to bed when I do— he's got work to finish up, he's tired, there's a late-night movie he wants to watch, and on and on. He told me over breakfast this morning that he has to go out of town this week. I've decided to hire an investigator to follow him."

"I'm sorry that it's come to this, Marisa, but I guess it's better to know for certain what's going on."

"I didn't call to discuss my wretched life, though. Did he stay?"

"No. He didn't even come inside, although I did invite him."

"Hmm. This calls for drastic action on your part."

Carina laughed. "You're incorrigible. You know that, don't you?"

"Just part of my charm."

"All right. Exactly what would you suggest?"

"Have him over for dinner this evening. Mom always sends you home from our Sunday get-togethers with enough to feed an army."

"I can do that."

"You don't want to be slaving over a hot stove before he comes, anyway. You want to take a long, refreshing bath. Use scented oil in the water. Have the place lit with candles, have soft music playing. You know, get him in the mood."

"Uh-huh."

"C'mon, you can do it. I have faith in you."

"I'm glad somebody does. You know I'm not very experienced. What did Al have to say about Jude after we left?"

"I think he likes him. At least he was talking about some of his relatives in politics, both here and in D.C."

"Of course Al would be interested in Jude's connections. Did he say anything about him, personally?"

"Just that he didn't show much ambition."

"Well, that's true. But I don't want to marry the guy. I'd just like to have an affair with him. I'm sure he could teach me a few things that would further my education a little."

"So. Are you going to invite him over tonight?"

"I'll ask him. I can't force him to come, you know."

"Go for it. You'll be glad you did."

"So you say."

* * *

Carina's call late Sunday morning surprised Jude. He hadn't expected to hear from her and he hadn't made any plans to see her. He'd been contemplating a visit to the ranch to see the new baby and visit with his parents and her unexpected suggestion caught him off guard.

"I thought you might like to come over this evening," she said. "There's a great lineup of movies on cable. I'd like to do something for you in exchange for all the time and money you've spent entertaining me since we met."

"Ah, I…"

"Please don't say no. We've been so busy attending various functions that we haven't had a chance for just the two of us to be together."

Which was why he knew he should say no.

"I'd really like to, Carina, b—"

"Good. I'll see you at seven, then," she said, and hung up.

Jude looked at the phone in his hand and heard the dial tone. "Well, that went well."

"You talking to yourself these days, Crenshaw?" John asked, ambling into the kitchen with a cup in his hand. He refilled his coffee and leaned against the counter.

"I must be. You know, there are times when this job really is the pits."

"Tell me about it. I never talk to myself. However, I have long, involved discussions with my computer. My Internet service provider and I discuss with a great deal of originality the ancestors of the people who've set up all the safeguards to protect the information I'm looking for."

Jude pulled out the makings of a sandwich from the refrigerator and made himself some lunch. "Does it help?"

"Oh, yeah. My blood pressure stays at a healthy level and I've yet to put my foot through the monitor. That's worth something."

"If I knew as much as you do about computers, I'd be more than willing to change jobs with you."

He carried his sandwich and glass of iced tea to the table.

John sat across from him. "You'd have me date the beauteous Carina? Man, oh, man. I'd do that in a heartbeat. You getting bored with her?"

"No. Just tired of this whole charade I'm playing. I want to get the evidence and get the hell out of here."

"As do we all, my friend. Maybe the trip to Mexico will net us what we're looking for."

"I can only live in hope."

"So what's on for today with Carina?"

"She invited me to dinner this evening at her apartment."

"I'm waiting to hear the bad part."

"That *is* the bad part. Now that we have the info on the brothers' next move, I don't need to see her so much. If they're out of town, there's no reason for me to date her now."

"So break up with her."

"I plan to, but not until we're sure we've got the necessary evidence to nail their hides to the wall. I want to get these guys and every one of the bastards selling drugs to kids."

"Maybe you should have been a DEA agent."

Jude chewed, swallowed and drank some tea. "Maybe. However, I like the job I'm doing now at NSA. Which reminds me, you guys have been awfully friendly to an outsider who came in and took over this investigation."

"You didn't 'take over.' You were put in charge because we knew we had to do something drastic after our friend was killed. We'd take orders from Attila the Hun to get results in this job."

"Attila. I'm flattered to be in such august company."

John laughed. "Actually, you're not half-bad. We figured you for some hotdogger who'd throw his weight and authority around us peons, but that hasn't happened. The consensus is that you're not half-bad to work with."

Jude laughed and finished his drink. He took his plate and glass over and put them in the dishwasher. "Wow. All this adulation is going straight to my head."

"Yeah, well, I guess I've stroked that ego of yours long enough. I'm going back to work."

"You could take the day off, you know. You're entitled."

"Maybe, but I'm more comfortable with computers than I am with people, anyway. Uh, present company excepted, of course."

"Of course. Goes without saying." Jude walked out of the kitchen with John. "You've inspired me to go take care of the piles of paperwork on my desk."

John laughed. "Don't you love this profession? A thrill a minute."

Jude knocked on Carina's door at seven o'clock, feeling virtuous. He'd worked all afternoon filling out reports, filing papers, reading the reports of each of the agents until he'd cleared his desk. He considered this evening to be on his own time. As such, it was his choice to spend the time however he wanted. Since it would have been rude to cancel, he showed up at her door at the time requested.

She opened the door and stepped back. The way her face lit up and her smile sparkled made him uneasy. Something about their relationship had shifted the night of the ballet and country-and-western music dance hall. She seemed to have opened up to him in a way he couldn't get a handle on. She'd told him that night that she liked him, which was fine, but he thought she'd also come to trust him, which wasn't so fine. He really didn't want to hurt Carina.

He'd first noticed her change of attitude toward him at the cookout yesterday, when she'd made it clear to all observers that they were a couple.

Once he stepped inside, she shut the door behind him. "I'm glad you could make it," she said, still smiling.

There was something different about her tonight. Different from yesterday, even. She wore a slip of a thing that stopped at her knees with spaghetti straps over her shoulders.

There was a hint of a scent about her that he couldn't place but he knew it wasn't her regular perfume, which was bad enough. But this, whatever it was, wrapped around him like a siren's song, promising him all kinds of delights if he'd move closer to her.

Instead he stepped away and looked around.

The light was muted on a dimmer switch. A couple of large pillar candles sat at either end of the coffee table. In between was a huge platter filled with finger food.

"You must have gone to a lot of work to get this ready."

"Not really. I hope you like it."

"Looks good."

"Have a seat. We can turn on the TV now or wait until a little later."

He sank into her comfortable couch and sighed. "Ah, feels good to relax."

"I could give you a backrub a little later, if you'd like."

This wasn't going well if he was trying to keep tonight casual and friendly. Of course she wasn't large enough to overpower him, but he definitely felt as though he was on the defensive.

On the other hand—and he had to be fair here—in the

normal course of dating, being together like this would be the next step in a budding relationship. He could hardly tell her the truth about why he'd been dating her, which meant he'd have to walk a very thin line. He had no intention of taking advantage of her.

So Jude found it impossible to explain to himself a few hours later exactly why they were on the sofa making out like a couple of teenagers.

They'd eaten and watched a movie that had more romance than action. In fact, there were some pretty steamy scenes that would stir anyone. When Carina turned to him and kissed him, it seemed natural to return the kiss and the caress.

When he finally paused for breath, Jude said, "Carina, I thought we were going to keep our relationship casual."

He really had trouble concentrating when she had her hands under his shirt. She had found his nipples and kept rubbing her fingers lightly across them. He didn't need any more stimulation.

She tilted her head back and looked at him, and then down the length of the sofa where she lay half on him, and then back at him. Her lips were puffy from their shared kisses. "This is casual, don't you think?"

Since his hand was pressed against her rear beneath the short skirt and the straps of her outfit had slid down her arms so that her breasts were exposed, he had trouble thinking.

"I mean," she went on, "we're certainly not dressed to go to a benefit or the ballet."

He rubbed his hand firmly up her spine, pressing her against him. "I mean, that if we don't stop this—right now—we're definitely going to be making love. Is that what you want?"

She looked at him with delight. "Oh, yes, that's exactly what I want!" She patted his cheek and added, "I promise to be gentle." Her sparkling eyes made him forget why he'd ever thought he should stop.

He held on to her and rolled to his feet, heading for the bedroom with her in his arms. "You're something else, you know that?" he said between kisses. He dropped her on the bed and she laughed. She removed the satiny looking slip-thing and he couldn't get out of his clothes fast enough.

He paused as he got into bed. "Damn. I wasn't planning on this happening."

She touched his erection lightly with her fingertip. "You forgot to tell *him* because he's ready to go."

"I don't have a condom with me and I don't want to—"

He stopped when she opened the drawer in the bedside table and handed him one.

He grinned. "You know, if I didn't know better, I would say you'd planned this."

"Really?" she replied, full of innocence. "Gee, what gave me away? The soft lighting, the music, the sexy movie or the fact that I only had one garment on?"

"I don't want you to be sorry," he finally said, carefully taking her into his arms.

"The only reason I might be sorry is if you decide to leave right now."

"It's too late for that, I'm afraid. I want you too badly."

Eight

Jude had her so hot and bothered that Carina shook with need. Was this what Marisa had meant when she'd teased her about her lack of experience? Carina had never felt such a need deep inside her to reach completion. She wanted to feel his hard body against her, to run her hands over his back to provoke a shiver in him, to hear his harsh breathing and know that he was as aroused as she was.

The heat of his body enhanced the faint scent of his aftershave and she knew in that moment that she would never forget Jude and his lovemaking.

Some restraint seemed to have snapped within him because Jude no longer hesitated. He appeared focused on bringing her to the edge of a whole new world.

He stretched out between her legs and nibbled on first one breast and then the other, his hands never stopping their soft caress of her body from her waist to her thighs. The jolt of pure desire wherever he touched her caused Carina to whimper with need, frantically reaching for him until he shifted and slipped inside her.

She moaned her satisfaction when he filled her and she lifted her legs around his hips. The shift in angle caused him to gasp and to thrust faster, causing her to explode unexpectedly into myriad pieces of heat and pleasure, her body clasping tightly around him in convulsive waves. He continued to move faster and faster until his whole body stiffened and he gave a muffled shout, surging inside her before he collapsed.

She fought for breath but he was too heavy. He shifted and rolled to his side, giving her a chance to draw in some much-needed air.

And then she smiled. She turned to face him. He lay with his eyes closed, which is when she noticed for the first time his long thick eyelashes. She wanted to touch him but didn't have the strength necessary to lift her hand, much less her arm.

When their breathing quieted, Jude opened his eyes and saw her watching him. He sighed and pulled her closer to him.

"This wasn't what this relationship was to be about," he said ruefully.

"I didn't realize there were rules we were following," she replied. "I don't see where anything has to change. If you're tired of me and want to date others, I can accept that."

He shook his head before she finished her sentence. "I'm not tired of you. It's just that…I'm not looking for a long-term relationship."

"Neither am I," she quickly replied. "I'm ready to get out into the world again. I don't want anything serious."

"Ah." For some reason, he didn't seem particularly pleased with her explanation.

"I wanted to make love with you. It's really no big deal."

He pulled away from her and frowned. "Thanks heaps."

She laughed. Whenever she tried to pause and explain a little better, she laughed harder. "I wasn't talking about you!" she managed to say. "I thought you'd be reassured to know I'm not ready to settle down."

"Oh. Well. I guess that's okay."

"I'm glad you think so." She brushed her mouth against his chest. "I hope you don't have to leave right away."

"No, I can stay." He got out of bed and headed toward the bathroom. "I'll be right back. Don't go away."

A little after six the next morning Jude quietly stepped into his kitchen from the garage. He figured everyone in the house would be asleep and he could slip upstairs without anyone knowing what time he got home.

He figured wrong. John, unshaven and with stubble on his face, stood in front of the coffeepot, watching the liquid drip into the carafe. They looked at each other in surprise. John was the first one to speak.

"I thought you were upstairs asleep."

"Yeah, well, what are you doing up so early?"

He placed a clean cup beside John's and waited until John poured them each some coffee.

"Haven't been to bed," John replied, sipping on the hot brew. "Looks like maybe you haven't—" he stopped. "Never mind," he said, and walked toward the hallway. "I'm going to bed."

"John?"

John looked over his shoulder. "Yeah?"

"I'd appreciate if you wouldn't say anything to the others."

John grunted. "I don't blame you. Since you're the only one getting laid these days, we might become a little testy around you."

"It isn't like that."

John turned and faced him. "Really. Then you didn't spend the night with Carina."

Jude pushed his hand through his hair. "It's complicated, okay?"

"Yeah, I can see where it might be, since the only reason you're seeing her is because of our investigation. She might be feeling a little used."

Jude was tired—he hadn't gotten all that much sleep last night—and he had to clamp down on his temper. "Look. We're both consenting adults. She's not looking for anything more from me than before. We know she's not a suspect, so it's not like I'm betraying anyone."

"Sounds reasonable. And logical. The only problem with that is that you're not thinking with your brain, Crenshaw, and we both know it. Sex changes things in a relationship. There's no way that it can't. Do you plan to tell Sam in your next report?"

"I doubt that he'd consider it any of his business."

"Really. You don't think he might be interested to learn that one of the men working for him has fallen for a member of the Patterson family?"

"You don't know what you're talking about. I haven't fallen for anybody, okay? I like her just fine. I enjoy being with her, just as she seems to enjoy being with me. This isn't about the assignment and you know it. Maybe you should get out and get laid and then you'd—" Jude stopped and dropped his head. "Okay, that was way out of line and I'm sorry. Look. We're both tired. Let's get some sleep and we can discuss it later."

John turned away. "As far as I'm concerned, there's nothing to discuss."

Jude watched him walk away and momentarily considered saying something, but the truth was, John was right. He'd spent the night with Carina. Talking wouldn't change that fact.

He'd slipped out of bed as dawn light filtered through the blinds. He'd looked down at her as she lay with her dark hair scattered across her pillow. The sheet had dropped away from her shoulders and her knee peeked out of the covers.

Jude would never admit to anyone how the night they'd just shared had affected him. Making love to Carina had been like nothing he'd ever experienced before. Or maybe his feelings had been different. He'd wanted her, sure, but he hadn't been prepared for the intensity or the fact that all she had to do was to touch him and he was hard.

If somewhere in his mind he figured that taking her to bed would get her out of his system, he'd been wrong. Very wrong. While he took a shower before going to bed his mind repeatedly replayed making love to her, her soft and delicate skin, the erotic scent she wore and hearing the sweet noises she made when he brought her to a climax. And he wanted her again.

Once in bed, Jude punched his pillow and buried his head in it. All right. Maybe he was more attracted to her than he liked, but he'd get over it. As soon as he returned to Maryland and got back into his usual routine, all of this would be a dull memory.

That evening Jude met with the other three agents to see what they'd found out.

Hal spoke first. "We're booked on a flight that leaves in the morning. We'll be in the terminal when the Pattersons get in. They've chartered a plane but still have to go through customs. We won't let them out of our sight. If they split up, so will we. Once we find out where they're staying we'll place bugs in their rooms."

"Is there any way you could place one somewhere on their clothing?" Jude suggested. "Say on a belt? Something they wear every day? I doubt they'll take extras."

"That's true," Ruth said. "Men have no style at all."

"So what do *you* intend to take for the trip, Ruth?" John asked.

"The very latest in fashion wear for tourists…bright shirts and skirts, a couple of pairs of slacks and a dandy array of wide-brimmed hats to keep the sun out of my face, don't you know." She batted her eyes at him.

"I think I've found a lead that may get us where we want to go," John said next. "One of the companies that the Pattersons pay monthly, listed under operating expenses, is a dummy corporation with several bank accounts. The money gets deposited to several accounts offshore. Now all I have to do is prove that part of the money went—or is still going to—Davies and Sullivan. If we can nail them on bribery charges, chances are they may break down and tell us what they know about the operation."

"And about the agent's death?" Jude asked.

"Let's just say we'll find out everything we need to know from them once they're arrested. At that point, they'll be eager to exonerate themselves with all kinds of explanations. A good one is 'it was either take the bribe or die.' Sometimes the choices are simple. But a good agent then turns around and reports it and gets the hell out of the area. These guys decided not to share their experience with the rest of the agency. It's also possible that Gregg refused the bribe and his decision got him killed."

"Let's hold off arresting them once you have proof until we've got the Pattersons in custody," Jude said. "If we get the date and time for the next shipment during your trip, we can be waiting in the warehouse when it comes. I definitely think things are heating up."

"Sounds good," John said. "I'm ready to wind this thing up, myself." There was a general murmur of agreement. He looked at Jude and asked, "So what are your plans for the week, Jude? Not much for you to do until we get everything in place."

"I may go spend a day or two with my family. It will be a good opportunity for me to do that while we're waiting for information."

Ruth said, "You aren't going to suddenly deprive your lady friend of your company, are you?"

"I may need to tell her that I'm seeing someone else and let the relationship end."

"That's unnecessarily cruel, don't you think?" she replied.

Jude had no idea how to end the relationship. "All right. You tell me. How am I going to end this thing without hurting her?"

"Well, that depends. I take it you haven't declared yourself to her, promised her a lifetime of happiness or anything like that?"

"No, I've done my best to keep things casual between us." He ignored John's sudden need to clear his throat.

"Then you see less of her. Visiting family is a good way to do that. You'll be out of town. Don't call her as often; don't ask her out as often and soon she'll realize that you've lost interest. It won't make it any easier for her because, let's face it, our egos are always involved, and nobody likes to be dumped, but at least you're not shoving her nose in it by telling her you're seeing someone else."

"Makes sense."

Ruth looked at him for a moment and said, "Don't tell

me you've never broken up with anyone before because I refuse to believe it."

"I've never gone into a relationship under false pretenses before. We always had a clear understanding of what we were looking for and what we wanted from the relationship. This is not the same."

"Too bad she isn't a part of all this. It might have been easier for you to arrest her!" Ruth said, half-kidding.

Jude shook his head in disgust. "That's not close to being funny." He looked at the other two. "Okay. We know what's happening this week. Keep in touch. Let me know when you'll be coming back. You have my cell number."

The others went in to watch television but Jude was too restless to concentrate. Instead he got into his car and drove back roads until late that night, listening to his favorite kind of music and convincing himself that he needed to forget Carina.

"What are your plans for tonight?" Marisa asked when Carina answered the phone Wednesday afternoon.

"Good question. Would you like to see a movie?"

There was a brief silence before Marisa said, "You mean you don't have a date?"

"Nope."

"Have you talked to him?"

"Not since Sunday. My skilled seduction scene must not have impressed him all that much. Haven't seen or heard from him since."

"Oh, Carina, I'm sorry. I know you really like him."

"Yes, I do, but I never had any illusions about the nature of our relationship. Didn't you tell me about his reputation when I first mentioned him?"

"I thought this was different. He spent so much more

time with you than he's ever spent with anyone else, that I'd hoped he was getting serious."

"Who can explain the way men's minds work? I'll stick with my music. I'll be moving to New York in another few weeks, anyway. I really don't need a relationship with anyone at the moment. He knew that at the very beginning and no doubt figures whatever we had has run its course." She paused, took a big breath and slowly exhaled before she said brightly, "So. Wanna see a movie?"

"You know, I think I will. Al's gone and my sister loves to keep the kids. It will be fun to have a girls' night out."

Once Carina hung up, she sat staring at the phone, irritated with herself. Since Monday, every time the phone rang she had dashed to pick it up in hopes that Jude was calling.

It was never him. And after three days, she needed to admit that she'd probably seen the last of him.

Was she really that bad in bed?

He'd seemed to enjoy her at the time. More than enjoy, considering the fact they got very little sleep that night. His stamina amazed her. She blushed at some of the memories from that night.

Her first disappointment Monday morning was when she woke up to find that all trace of him was gone. She'd looked for a note, something, to say he'd call her later, but found nothing.

The next day she'd tried to think of a reason to call him but realized that he would see through whatever excuse she might use. She needed to come to terms with the fact that he'd taken what she so freely offered, but their night together obviously didn't mean anything to him.

What had she expected, anyway? She'd wanted to make love with him. She'd made love with him. What more did she want?

She refused to look at possible answers to that question. Instead, she got ready to meet Marisa.

For the past three days Jude had picked up the phone to call Carina more times than he could count. Now it was Wednesday. He hadn't heard from Hal and Ruth since they'd arrived in Mexico and he was wearing out the rug in his bedroom.

He wanted to call her. Hell, he needed to call her and to see her. Was she all right? What was she thinking about the way he'd left her asleep without a word or a note? No doubt she was royally ticked and he couldn't blame her. He was convinced this was the better way. She'd probably be so angry by the time he called her that she'd refuse to see him again. The truth was that there was no graceful way to end the relationship. None of the usual reasons made any sense.

He decided to drive to the ranch and visit with his family for a few hours.

Being in the Hill Country always managed to soothe him. The two-hour drive helped him to detach from his present assignment, and by the time he turned into the entrance of the ranch, he was smiling in anticipation of seeing everyone again.

He eventually reached the main ranch house where Jake and Ashley lived. Once parked, he sat and stared at the home where he'd grown up. The thick, cream-colored adobe walls and red-tile roof had housed several generations of Crenshaws. It had been modernized over the years and despite its size, had a comfortable air about it.

His mom and dad had built a smaller home on the ranch five miles or so from Jake when his dad retired from ranching several years ago. Jude was glad that someone had been willing to stay home and run the ranch because he certainly didn't want to. He'd had enough of hard labor, blistering heat, dirt and blowing sand and sweat running off his face while he was growing up.

Of course he'd experienced hard labor, blistering heat, dirt and blowing sand and sweat running off his face many times while he was in the army. However, he had much preferred the military to riding horseback, trying to herd cattle or worse, attempting to herd sheep.

Jude opened the car door, got out and stretched. Then he walked toward the patio nearest to the kitchen. When he stepped on the concrete slab, he heard the door open and saw Jake in the doorway with a huge grin on his face.

"I can't believe it! You actually tore yourself away from all your fun down in San Antonio to come see us." He stepped outside and greeted Jude with a big hug. "It's great to see you. Do the folks know you were coming?"

"No. I wasn't sure if they were back from their latest trip." He stepped back and eyed Jake. "Looks like you survived your son's birth. How are he and Ashley doing?"

Jake opened the door and waved Jude through. "They're both doing great. They've been home a few days now and we're learning how to deal with an infant's schedule. Ashley will be thrilled to see you."

Once inside, Jude helped himself to the coffee that was always ready. He held up the pot in a silent question and Jake shook his head. "I've had enough. We were up at one-thirty this morning and again at three. I've probably consumed a whole pot of the stuff since then."

Now that Jake mentioned it, Jude noticed his brother's bloodshot eyes for the first time. In the past he would have figured that Jake was suffering from a hangover. Now it was because of his newborn son.

Time has a way of changing all kinds of things in a person's life.

As though he were talking to himself, Jake mumbled, "I'm amazed that something that small can make so much noise. He could wake the dead when he's hungry."

"Guess you're going to have to take catnaps during the day to keep up with him."

Jake snorted. "Oh, sure. I can see that now, can't you? I'll give the crew their orders, then curl up beneath a tree somewhere and snooze while they work. That'd really go over."

"Where's Ashley now, asleep?"

"She was nursing him when I came downstairs. She's worrying that her milk may not be rich enough to satisfy him."

"Whoa, whoa, whoa. That's way more information than I need, bro. Now you've got me thinking about Ashley's breasts. Let's don't even go there!"

Jake smiled wryly. "Remember, all this is brand-new to me and I'm having a crash course in being around an infant. I didn't see Heather until she was almost four. These tiny guys are a complete mystery to me."

Jude leaned against the cabinet and sipped his coffee. "I can tell you're loving every minute of being the father of a newborn, aren't you?"

Jake laughed. "Yeah, I am. Do you want to see him?"

Jude shifted in alarm. "Not if he's feeding."

"I'll make sure you aren't scarred for life by seeing an infant breastfeed, okay?"

Jude put his cup on the counter and followed Jake into the large foyer where the wide staircase gracefully curved up to the second floor. As they walked down the hallway, Jude said, "I just realized what's different about the place. I don't hear a little girl talking nonstop. Where's Heather?"

"She's in town visiting one of her friends...the grand-

The Silhouette Reader Service™ — Here's how it works:

Accepting your 2 free books and gift places you under no obligation to buy anything. You may keep the books and gift and return the shipping statement marked "cancel." If you do not cancel, about a month later we'll send you 6 additional books and bill you just $3.80 each in the U.S., or $4.47 each in Canada, plus 25¢ shipping and handling per book and applicable taxes if any.* That's the complete price and — compared to cover prices of $4.50 each in the U.S. and $5.25 each in Canada — it's quite a bargain! You may cancel at any time, but if you choose to continue, every month we'll send you 6 more books, which you may either purchase at the discount price or return to us and cancel your subscription.

*Terms and prices subject to change without notice. Sales tax applicable in N.Y. Canadian residents will be charged applicable provincial taxes and GST. Credit or debit balances in a customer's account(s) may be offset by any other outstanding balance owed by or to the customer.

GET FREE BOOKS and a FREE GIFT WHEN YOU PLAY THE...

SLOT MACHINE GAME!

Just scratch off the silver box with a coin. Then check below to see the gifts you get!

YES! I have scratched off the silver box. Please send me the 2 free Silhouette Desire® books and gift for which I qualify. I understand I am under no obligation to purchase any books, as explained on the back of this card.

326 SDL D7WS

225 SDL D7W6

FIRST NAME	LAST NAME

ADDRESS

APT.#	CITY

STATE/PROV.	ZIP/POSTAL CODE

DETACH AND MAIL CARD TODAY!

daughter of Ashley's receptionist. We thought it would make this transition a little easier if Heather could be entertained somewhere for a few hours each day. Luckily, she loved the idea."

"Did you ever agree on a name for your son?" Jude asked at the same time the bedroom door opened and Ashley stepped into the hallway. She had on a cotton housecoat and looked pretty good, considering what she'd gone through recently.

"Jude!" she exclaimed, hugging him around the waist. "It's so good to see you. And yes, our son has a name."

"Which is?"

She leaned back slightly and met his gaze. "Joseph Kenneth Crenshaw. He's named after both his grandfathers."

"Okay, the hug's gone on long enough," Jake growled impatiently. "It's time to introduce you to Joey."

Ashley stepped away from Jude and smiled sweetly at her husband. "If you wake him up, you get to put him back to sleep."

"Or…maybe we'll wait for him to wake up on his own. If last night was any indication that won't be too long," Jake replied, rolling his eyes.

Jude draped his arm around Ashley's shoulder and the three of them went downstairs. He could almost hear Jake grinding his teeth as he followed behind them. Jude grinned. Jake was as possessive as ever of Ashley, which was why he enjoyed tweaking him about it.

When they sat at the table Jake made sure he was the one next to Ashley. Jude winked at her and she laughed.

"What's so funny?" Jake asked her.

"Oh, you know Jude. He's making funny faces at me again."

"Why is it the two of you make me feel so old?"

Ashley rested her head on his shoulder. "Believe me, you aren't close to being old."

"Are the folks in town?" Jude asked quickly, unwilling to listen if Ashley decided to go into detail.

"They came back early. Got here a couple of days before Joey was born. I think Ashley decided to wait for them to get here before she gave birth."

She gave him an incredulous stare before looking at Jude. "Oh, sure, that's what I did, all right. Being the size of a horse, waddling everywhere—not to mention what an active baby can do to a bladder—was way too much fun to give up too soon."

"Ah," Jude replied. He couldn't think of anything else to say.

Jake grinned, no doubt at his obvious discomfort. "Just wait until you're married, old son, and you'll have the opportunity to learn firsthand what she's talking about."

"I think I'll pass," Jude replied quickly, annoyed that thoughts of Carina popped into his head. "I'm going to let you and Jared fulfill any family obligations we have to the next generation. Speaking of Jared, how are they doing?"

"They're looking for a house to buy somewhere near Houston," Ashley replied. "Lindsey wants a large place with lots of lawn area for the children she wants to have. She doesn't want to raise an only child, having been one herself."

The three of them visited another hour before Joey let his presence be known. Jude was amused at the immediate response to his cry. He trailed Jake and Ashley into their bedroom and walked over to a baby bed set in an alcove of the room. Ashley picked up the crying infant and snuggled him into the curve of her shoulder and neck.

"Wow. He's really small," Jude finally said. "I've seen newborn puppies bigger than that."

Ashley nodded and spoke softly, so she wouldn't startle Joey. "So have I, for that matter. But he's plenty big enough and he's healthy."

Jake absently placed his hand on Joey's back, his fingers resting against the baby's neck, his palm cupping his bottom. The look Jake and Ashley shared was so intimate that Jude felt they were no longer aware he was there.

He realized with something of a shock that he envied them.

While Joey ate, Jake called their mom and dad and told them that Jude was visiting. They arrived in fifteen minutes. His mom clung to him for a moment and said, "I've missed hearing from you. And seeing you."

"I'm here now, Mom," he said, and draped an arm around her, shaking his dad's hand with the other.

"How long can you stay?" Joe asked.

"I figure I'll head back this afternoon. But that still gives us most of the day to visit."

And visit they did. He heard all about their latest trip—where they'd gone, who they'd met and what they'd seen. Gail and Ashley prepared lunch and Joey joined them for another brief visit after lunch before Ashley took him upstairs to sleep.

Jude visited with Joe and Jake and continued to relax as the day passed. When he reluctantly took his leave, he promised them that he'd be back before much longer and would be able to stay a week or so.

He was in a much better mood when he reached the San Antonio city limits than he had been when he'd left. He looked at the time. It was early, around seven. He decided to drop by Carina's, casual-like, and get the lay of the land there. She might close the door in his face, for all he knew, but he wanted to see her again.

Just to say hi.

He knocked on her door a couple of times before he had to face the fact that she wasn't at home. He turned and surveyed the parking lot, but didn't see her car. Not that it made a difference. She could be on a date, for all he knew.

Which irritated him. He'd spent Sunday night with her and by Wednesday she was out with someone else? He reminded himself that nothing she did was any of his business.

Maybe she was visiting her parents. That was probably it. He'd give her a call the next day and see if she'd like to get out for a few hours.

They were friends, after all. Friends could spend an hour or two together without a problem.

Nine

Carina practiced the piano a minimum of four hours a day and had done so for many years. Since the weekend she had spent most of her time working on her music. She found that the concentration needed helped keep the pain of Jude's defection away.

When the phone interrupted her, Carina looked at the clock. She'd been playing for almost three hours.

This time she knew it wasn't going to be Jude. She tried to convince herself that she no longer cared.

"Hello?"

"Hi."

The sound of his voice destroyed all coherent thought. Had his voice always sounded to deep? She put her hand over her chest in hopes of calming her racing pulse.

Finally, she said, "Hello, Jude," and sank onto the sofa.

"I—uh—I thought I'd see how you're doing."

"Quite well, thank you."

"Good." Pause. "That's good." Longer pause. "I went to visit my family this week. Got back yesterday evening."

So he'd been out of town. That still didn't excuse his rudeness. "I'm sure they were pleased to see you. You saw the baby?"

"Yes. Yes, I did. He, uh, he looks like a, uh, baby. They say he's healthy, which is good."

"Why are you calling?" she asked.

He cleared his throat. "I guess I left a little abruptly Monday morning."

"You guess, but you're not sure."

"The truth is…the real truth is that— Aw, hell. Forget it. Sorry I disturbed you."

"Jude! Wait."

"What?"

"Would it help if we saw each other and talked out what happened?"

"It happened. There's nothing to talk about, except that I want to make love to you so badly I ache all the time. I've been in this condition since I left you. I'm not blaming you. It's just that—" A long pause. "I know we didn't intend for our relationship to become this involved. As a matter of fact, it looks like I'll be leaving San Antonio before much longer."

Carina felt a pain in her chest and forced herself to breathe. She'd known all along that nothing could come of their dating other than enjoying his company while she could. So why did the news that he was leaving hurt so?

"Oh?" she said after a lengthy pause. "Where will you go?"

No answer.

"Jude?"

"I, um, I'm not sure just yet. I'll be spending time with my family and then I'm thinking about going east and looking up an old army buddy I haven't seen in a long while."

"I see."

"I know you're going to New York soon."

"That's right."

"The thing is, I really want to see you again. There's no hidden agenda. I enjoy spending time with you. I mean, we'll both head east in a few weeks, anyway. Do you have a problem continuing to see me until then?"

"I wasn't the one who left Monday morning."

"Right. Guess I was a coward for not telling you goodbye."

"I'm not certain of the etiquette in that kind of situation, but it seems that would be the polite thing to do."

"I'm sorry."

She smiled. "Apology accepted."

"Great. Thanks. Would you like to do something today? Maybe have lunch or something?"

"I keep wondering what the 'or something' is."

He laughed. "I'm trying to be polite here."

"Jude. Come over and we'll decide on the something we'd like to do today."

"'Bye."

Carina couldn't believe he'd practically hung up on her and she chuckled.

Okay. So she was an idiot. She had no business seeing him again and she knew it. She was too vulnerable where Jude was concerned. Their night together taught her so much about herself and her perspective and just how wrong she'd been about sex.

She realized that she knew next to nothing about making love or how to please a man. She and Danny had been friends, first and foremost. They were comfortable with each other but there had never been the sexual spark between them that had occurred the first time she met Jude.

For the first time she could better understand what Danny must have known about their relationship. It explained why he'd been seeing someone else. If he'd only been honest with her. But back then she wouldn't have understood.

Now she did. And she forgave him.

What she felt when she was with Jude was so much more. She was aware of him constantly; everything he did, every move he made. She knew his voice and his laugh and the way he whispered endearments when he made love to her.

Of course he didn't say that he loved her. She would never want him to lie to her. He'd been honest and up-front about who he was from the very beginning, which is why she'd learned to trust him. She knew that Jude would never intentionally hurt her. She found the thought comforting.

She discovered that she wanted to continue to see him while they were in San Antonio. She wanted to gather memories of him. No one could hurt those memories and she would look back on this time in her life with joy. She would move on and meet someone else and be happy, but she knew that she would never, not ever, forget Jude Crenshaw.

When Jude knocked on the door, she opened it and smiled at him. "Come on in."

He placed his hand against the doorjamb and leaned on it. "I'd rather not. Let's get something to eat. There's this great little place on the River Walk that I like. Then this afternoon I thought we might go over to Fiesta Texas and see what that's all about. This evening we can go to Crazy Eights if you're up for it."

"Wow. That's quite an itinerary. All public places. How interesting."

He grinned. "I'm hoping I can keep my hands off you."

She laughed. "That will be tough if we're going to be dancing the night away."

"You know what I mean. Are you up for it?"

She looked down at her slacks and sleeveless blouse. "I'm not certain this is appropriate to wear."

"It's perfect." He looked up and down the hallway before he looked back at her, almost bashfully. "So would you like to go have lunch?"

"I'd like that. I'll get my purse. If you don't want to come in—"

"I never said that! It's just that my willpower is a little shaky at the moment."

"You know, that's the best compliment anyone has ever paid me. You make me feel absolutely irresistible."

He waited a moment and then asked, "So where were you last night?"

She had walked over to pick up her purse on the kitchen bar. Now, she spun around and looked at him in surprise. Without saying anything, Carina moved toward him, pausing to make certain the door locked behind her, and then looked at him.

"I, uh, came by when I got back into town and you weren't here." He walked beside her with his hands in his pockets.

"Is that right?"

"Uh-huh."

"Then I was obviously out."

"I know that."

"And you think my whereabouts is any of your business because—?"

"Sorry," he mumbled. "I really missed you and…I hope you had a good time."

"Oh, I did."

"Mmm."

She laughed. "Jude, for someone who insists that there are no strings attached in this relationship, you're sounding a tad jealous."

"I know. I'm confused as hell about how I'm feeling, myself. I have no doubt that you'll put me in my proper place whenever I step over the line."

They reached the car and he opened the door for her.

When he got in and started the car, she said, "What kind of restaurant do you have in mind?"

"It's called Boudro's and they serve some of the best Cajun food you can find outside of Louisiana. Of course, if that's too spicy for you, they have other things on the menu, as well." He glanced at her out of the corner of his eye before he added, "And they make terrific margaritas, if you're so inclined."

She laughed. "It's a little early for that, but your choice sounds fine."

They followed Jude's agenda for the day. After lunch they drove to Fiesta Texas and wandered around looking at all the rides, trying a couple and in general enjoying the festive mood there.

They left in the late afternoon. As she leaned back in the passenger seat of Jude's car, Carina said, "Ah, this air-conditioning feels great. I didn't realize how tired I was until I sat down." She looked over at him. "Could we go to Crazy Eights another night?"

"Of course."

"I can't remember when I've had so much fun acting like a kid, riding the rides, trying for prizes. But my training wheels are dragging. Why don't we go back to my place and I'll make something light for supper. Maybe omelets, if you like them."

"I'm so glad you're ready to call it a day," Jude said, grinning. "I'm ready to take it easy for the rest of the evening. You know," he said earnestly, "a shower would help to cool us off once we get to your place."

"That's true."

"So I was thinking. We could conserve water and shower together, maybe?"

She exploded into laughter at his obvious suggestion that they get naked together. She saw absolutely nothing wrong with the idea. When she finally ran down, she smiled at him and said, "You know, Jude, I had no idea you were so ecology-minded."

Jude left Carina's apartment a little after midnight. This time he roused her enough to let her know he was leaving. The memory of her sleepy murmur and kiss kept him smiling to himself all the way to his house.

When Jude got home, he looked for John but the agent wasn't downstairs, so he went upstairs, went to bed and, for the first time since the weekend, slept deeply.

The phone woke him up at six the next morning.

"Crenshaw."

"We're at the airport. Can you pick us up?" Hal asked.

"I'm on my way."

Jude backed out of the garage five minutes later. Traffic was light at that time of the morning. Since the airport was on the north side of the city, he made good time heading south into town. Hal and Ruth were waiting near the curb when he pulled up in front of the international terminal. Jude helped them stow their luggage. "You should have called me earlier and I would have been here when you landed."

"There wasn't time. When we realized the brothers were flying back last night we caught the last available flight before morning," Ruth said, settling into the back seat.

"Was the trip worthwhile?" Jude asked, pulling away from the curb.

Hal answered, "If you mean, do we know when the stuff is coming in, then the trip was definitely worthwhile. The truck left some time yesterday evening. They expect it to arrive late tomorrow night."

"Did you find out how they transport it to get past the border?"

"They're shipping what looks like solid wood furniture, supposedly valuable antiques from Portugal. I managed to get a peek so that I'd recognize which furniture to zero in on."

"Then we've got them."

Jude waited until after lunch to call Carina. When she answered, he asked, "How did you sleep last night?"

She chuckled. "Funny thing. I managed to get much more sleep once you left."

"Not surprising. I have a tendency to pull covers."

"Or toss them. How are you?"

"Great." He was, too. Adrenaline was already pumping through his system. "Are you up for spending the evening practicing dance steps?"

"I'd love to."

"I've got errands to run and things to do until about eight this evening. The band doesn't start playing until nine. I'll pick you up a little after eight, if that's okay."

"See you then."

Carina hung up with a pleased smile on her face. She was going to enjoy each moment she spent with him without looking ahead to the future.

A little later the phone rang again and she thought it might be Jude. Instead, Marisa called.

"How are you?" she asked Marisa.

"Al's back."

"Is that good or bad?"

"He seemed preoccupied. Barely acknowledged my presence. I believe I'll drive up to Dallas and visit with my mother. I may put the kiddos in school there. This isn't a marriage, Carina. I don't know what it is anymore. All I know is the children and I shouldn't be treated like nonentities."

"Are you going to tell him why you're going?"

"No. I doubt he'll know we're gone for a few days. He got home late last night and was gone by seven this morning. Said he didn't know when he'd be home."

"Did you hire an investigator?"

"No. I figured what's the point? It doesn't really matter what he does with his time. It's obvious he doesn't want to spend it with me."

"Oh, Marisa, I'm so sorry all this is happening."

"Yeah, me, too. You may be losing a sister, but you'll never lose your friend."

"Thank goodness. Keep in touch, okay?"

"Absolutely. Let me give you my mother's phone number and you already have my cell phone. Who knows how long I'll have that?"

"Be sure to see a lawyer as soon as you get up there."

"I will. First thing Monday I'll make an appointment with one. And—Carina, let's don't tell your folks just yet."

"Wouldn't dream of it. This is your business. I never discuss it."

Marisa sounded choked up when she said, "Thank you. Take care now," and hung up.

Carina loved her brother dearly but realized as she got

older that neither he nor Benito deserved the pedestals she'd placed them on when she was a child. What she wanted to do was to take a bat to Alfredo and knock some sense into him. He loved his kids. She knew that. And he truly loved Marisa…or he had at one time.

She was glad that her affair with Jude was clearly defined. She would always have her music and fond memories without getting her heart broken.

"Friday night at the Crazy Eights once again," Carina said when the music greeted them as they pulled into the parking lot. "I forgot my earplugs!"

He patted his pocket. "I didn't." They both grinned at each other.

Carina had gone shopping that afternoon and wore what looked like the uniform of the rest of the patrons—tight jeans and Western-style shirt—but she balked at wearing boots. The shoes she'd chosen were low-heeled and comfortable.

There were no available tables. Jude found an empty spot against the wall and held Carina in front of him, his arms around her waist. After several minutes of watching for a table, Jude asked, "Do you want to dance?" in her ear.

She nodded. "Might as well."

They danced several dances before they went to the bar for something to drink. Tonight Carina chose a popular cola drink, which amused him.

"And here I thought I was going to have the pleasure of pouring you into bed again," he said, toasting her with his beer.

"Not a chance. I want to be wide awake and fully aware any time I get you into my bedroom."

He almost sprayed beer. Instead, he choked, coughed

and tried to laugh all at the same time. "I never know what you're going to say next."

"Good. Keeps you off balance. I like that in a man."

By midnight they were ready to go. Jude spent hours that night tenderly loving her, bringing her to the brink of satisfaction before starting over. When he finally moved to claim her, she felt liberated from reality. She soared in a new universe of sensual pleasure that she never wanted to end.

He waited for her to climax and then rolled over so that she was on top of him while he was still inside her. He sat her up, pulling her knees next to his sides and let her set the pace.

She felt such a sense of power and control as she moved seductively against him. When he could no longer stand her slow and teasing pace, he put his hands on her hips and moved her faster against him, his hips meeting hers in rapid strokes until they went over the edge together, floating in the sensual haze of satisfaction.

When Jude got up a few hours later, she roused and asked, "Why don't you stay the night?"

"Some other time, I promise," he said, reaching for his pants. "I'd like to see you tonight, if it's all right. However, I'll be late getting here. So if you'd rather forget about it, I understand."

"No, that's all right. I'd like you to come. So. You have another date earlier in the evening."

He pulled his shirt over his head before answering. "No. It's nothing like that. I have some business that needs to be completed. I'll tell you all about it when I get back here." He leaned over and gave her a long, tender and very loving kiss. When he straightened, he said, "Get some rest."

He walked out of the room without looking back.

Ten

The next day, each agent took his or her turn keeping watch over the Patterson warehouse. Hal had been inside enough that he could draw a map of the place and where inventory sat.

They needed to get inside not only before the shipment arrived but before the brothers arrived.

The four of them sat in a rented van and watched as workers left when their shift ended. A half hour later, the two brothers came outside and went to their cars.

"What do you think?" Hal asked. "According to my count, all the hired help has left."

"If you're wrong, we blow the bust," John reminded him.

"Hell, I know that!"

Ruth said calmly, "We're all on edge, guys. We know just how important this is. Don't take your nerves out on everybody else, okay?"

"What's the deal with Davies and Sullivan?" Jude asked.

John answered. "I alerted Sam that we've got the proof they accepted bribes. He has agents from the Virginia office standing by to make certain they don't skip out of town. He understands that we want in on the arrest."

"Hal," Jude said. "You know the interior of the building best. Check it out. If it's clear, signal. If you run into anybody, give them your homeless story and get the hell out of there."

Hal pulled on the coveralls that hid his regular clothes. They were stained and dirty. He'd let his hair grow out a little these last several weeks and he hadn't shaved in a couple of days. He was good at what he did and Jude had no doubt he could protect himself in the event he discovered someone was still inside the warehouse.

Twenty minutes later, Hal signaled an all clear. The rest of them slipped inside the warehouse and found places to hide until the truck arrived. It was going to be a long night. Waiting was always the worst when adrenaline kept pumping. Agents had to deal with the fear factor on a regular basis and each had his or her way of doing so.

Jude sat with his back against a wall. He was blocked from view on three sides and yet he had a clear view of the door to the loading dock. He blanked out of his mind everything but the job he had to do. The assignment could end tonight…successfully if the cocaine was actually delivered and unsuccessfully if there was nothing there and they were spotted.

He leaned his head against the wall, closed his eyes and waited.

"Benito! I wasn't expecting to see you here tonight," Al said, his voice echoing in the vast warehouse later that night. "I figured you'd be home sound asleep."

Jude and the other three agents watched and listened from the deep shadows.

"Yeah, I went to bed, but couldn't sleep. I figured I'd come down and wait with you."

Al looked at his watch. "The driver reported in once he cleared the border. If he didn't have any problems, he should be arriving at any time."

Jude felt his gut tighten when the rumbling of a semi announced that the merchandise had arrived.

Showtime.

He watched the trailer being unloaded. Hal had described the furniture in detail. He was a hell of an agent and deserved a promotion. Al paid the driver and waved him off before he lowered the wide door to the dock.

Without a word, the brothers carefully uncrated and unpacked each piece of furniture, pulling bags of cocaine from several of them. They worked steadily until they'd filled a good-size trash bag with dope. Jude waited until Al picked up the bag, ready to leave, before he stepped out of his hiding place with his hands behind him.

"How's it going, guys?" he asked. "No rest for the wicked, eh? Or is it no rest for the weary?"

Ben stared at him as though seeing a ghost. Al spun around and said, "What the hell are you doing here? And where were you?"

Jude nodded to where he'd been hidden without taking his eyes off Al. "Same thing you are, I'd imagine." He continued to walk toward Al while speaking. When he stopped, he dropped his arms, holding his pistol in one hand, his ID and badge out for Al to inspect.

"NSA! What's going on here?"

Ben looked over Al's shoulder at the ID and then at Jude. "You're a government agent?" he asked, sounding shocked.

"Boy, they must be scraping the bottom of the barrel if they hired you."

Jude signaled the others who stepped into the light and surrounded the men. Ruth began to tell them their rights.

"Maybe you'll be a little more impressed with these agents," he said, and turned away. "Let's get them in the van and down to federal headquarters. Make certain that under no circumstances are they to leave. We'll ask the judge on Monday not to offer bond. They're definite flight risks."

Hal and Ruth handcuffed and leg-shackled the brothers while John moved the van to the exit door. The four agents helped the Pattersons to navigate the steps from the office door without falling.

Once inside the van, Hal contacted the two men watching Davies and Sullivan. He reported a successful bust and told them that he, Ruth and John would be there within the hour.

They took the Pattersons to the federal building and booked them. Since no one in the local area had been notified of the impending raid, there were several shocked expressions when the Patterson brothers showed up in custody.

As soon as his part was done, Jude went outside where he'd left his car earlier and drove to Carina's. It was now two o'clock in the morning.

Carina roused slowly to the sound of repeated knocking. She'd fallen asleep on the couch waiting for Jude. She jumped up and ran to the door. "Jude?"

"Yeah. It's me."

She glanced at the time and opened the door. "I didn't expect you to be this la—" She stopped talking as soon as she saw him.

He wore a suit with the collar open and he looked grim.

"What's wrong? What happened?" she asked as he stepped inside.

"Would you mind making some coffee? I'll explain everything to you."

She turned away and made coffee. When she turned back he sat across the kitchen bar from her. He'd removed his coat. He wore a shoulder holster.

"Wha—? Why are you—?"

He flipped open a small wallet and slid it in front of her. She picked it up and studied the badge and ID card. "You work for the National Security Agency?" she asked in wonder.

He nodded. "This is the first time that I could tell you."

"Because you've been working on a case?"

"That's right. We finished our part of it tonight."

She blinked in confusion. "Who are we?"

"Three other agents I've been working with."

"Oh." She turned away and poured them both coffee, carried the cups around the bar and sat next to him. "Wow. This is really a shock. I don't know what to say."

"You don't have to say anything. I'd just appreciate it if you'd hear me out."

"Certainly. I mean, if you were working on a big case you probably weren't allowed to talk about it."

He nodded. "Exactly."

She smiled. "But now that it's over you can tell me. Thank you for being so up-front with me." She wondered why he looked grimmer now that he'd told her the truth.

"At the moment I'm not working for the NSA. I was loaned to the Drug Enforcement Administration…the DEA." He drank some coffee. "There's been a heavy flow of cocaine coming up from Mexico to San Antonio for distribution for some time now. It had to be stopped."

"It's truly evil, I know," she replied. "The papers are full of stories about the number of people addicted to drugs. And the children! What kind of evil person would sell to grade-school children and teenagers?"

"Greed is a powerful motive, sometimes. It's hard to predict who will fall prey to the need for money. One of the agents working on this case last year was killed. We think it's because he found out how the stuff was getting into the country and another agent who'd been bribed killed him or set him up to be killed. That's why I was brought in. My training has been in covert operations, although I haven't done that kind of work for a while. The DEA office in D.C. discovered that I'm a native Texan and they decided to use me because no one in the local DEA office would know I was a government agent."

"That makes sense." She leaned over and kissed him. "But it's over now. Does this mean you'll actually stay in bed this time instead of rushing away?" she teased. She stroked the hand that held his cup. "This must have been very stressful for you." She paused, and said, "So you do have a job and some ambition. Not that it mattered to me but Al harped on your playboy image. He's really going to be surprised."

He was, believe me. Out loud, Jude said, "There's something else you need to know."

"Okay, and then I want to go to bed. It's the middle of the night, you know. We can discuss all of this tomorrow." She smiled. "So you really are Superman beneath your Clark Kent exterior. How exciting."

He flinched as though she had slapped him.

"Your fiancé didn't have anyone with him when he was forced off the road and killed."

That was the last thing she would have guessed he had

to tell her. Danny was alone? Then why would her brothers tell her— Wait a minute. "You mean someone else caused the accident?"

"Yeah. I think we'll know who it was in the coming weeks."

"Oh, no! Are you saying that Danny was part of a smuggling operation? I can't believe that he would— But then, how do you know who will succumb to the temptation?"

"He wasn't a part of the smuggling. He found out who was and it got him killed."

Tears filled her eyes. "Instead of cheating on me he was trying to do the right thing."

"That's what we think, yes. At least, the smugglers didn't want to take any chances he'd talk."

"Do you know who was behind all this?"

"Yes." He turned and took her hand. She felt cold and her hand trembled and he knew that hearing about Dan had been a tremendous shock to her. "Here, you're cold. Let's get you into bed."

"Great. Now you want to go to bed after dropping that little bombshell on me." She tried to laugh but her voice shook too much.

He led her into the bedroom and searched her closet until he found a fleece-lined robe stuck in the far back. He pulled it out and put it around her.

"Thanks," she said through chattering teeth. "I don't know what's the matter with me."

"You've gone into shock and I'm so sorry to have caused it. I thought you needed to know the truth."

"Oh. Well. You couldn't know." She pulled him toward the bed and sat down. He sat and put his arms around her.

"Let me make you some hot tea."

"No, that's okay. You holding me is all that I need at the

moment." She laid her head on his chest. He squeezed his eyes shut and tried to swallow around the large lump that had formed in his throat.

She sighed after a while and sat up. "Thank you for telling me about Danny. You could have let me continue to believe that he'd been cheating on me, but you didn't. I'm sorry I didn't handle the news better."

"Don't apologize. None of this is your fault."

"I don't understand why my brothers would make up lies about him, though. I'm going over to Al's in the morning and demand an answer."

"You don't need to, Carina. I can tell you. Your brothers were arrested and taken into custody tonight. They were caught with a shipment of cocaine that arrived from Mexico. The evidence is irrefutable."

She stared at him blankly. "My brothers? You arrested my brothers?"

He nodded.

She straightened, then stood. "For smuggling? You've got to be kidding. If this is some kind of a joke I don't find it funny! Al and Ben would never— They couldn't be— I mean, this is unbelievable." She sat down again like a marionette whose strings had been cut. Slowly she turned her head and looked at him. "You saw them with it?"

He nodded.

"Did you know what they were doing when you came here?"

"We were fairly certain, but without evidence we couldn't stop them."

"So you came to San Antonio to get evidence. You said that earlier. Your purpose for living here was to catch my brothers smuggling."

She spoke calmly. Too calmly. He had known she'd

take this news hard, but he'd wanted to be the one to tell her exactly what had happened, rather than for her to hear some form of the story from someone else or read about the arrest in the local paper.

"As I mentioned, several of us have been working on this assignment."

Her color had returned for a while, but now her skin looked paper-white. Her stark gaze convicted him." That's why you've been seeing me, isn't it? You've been gathering evidence against my family while pretending to be interested in me."

"I didn't have to pretend interest, Carina. You fascinated me from the moment I met you. Regardless of my assignment, I would have wanted to get to know you better."

"Ah. Wanted to. But you wouldn't have asked me out if my name hadn't been Patterson."

"I'm not going to lie to you, Carina."

"Really? That would certainly be different." She stood. "I think you need to leave, unless you have another confession to make. If that's the case, tell me and go." She looked at her watch. "I need to go to my parents so I'll be there when they wake up. I need to prepare them as well as I can." Her face crumpled for a moment. She bit her bottom lip until she got some control over her emotions. "Sara's pregnant. What's this going to do to her and Beth? And Marisa?" A tear escaped. "She and the children left for Dallas."

He stood and reached for her. She stepped nimbly away. "Please show me the courtesy of not touching me."

"Everything that has gone on between you and me has been real, Carina. Yes, I was supposed to meet you and I did. You should know that at one time your entire family was suspected of being part of the operation."

"Well, that explains it. You needed a pretext to get into my apartment. I'm curious to know how you managed to do it without my knowing it. Was it last Monday morning when I slept so blissfully before you left?"

"I knew that you weren't a suspect before I ever made love to you."

"How noble of you." She turned her back. "Please get out of here. If you have any respect for me, any at all, then you will leave and never contact me again."

"My getting emotionally involved with you was not part of any plan, Carina. If you believe nothing else, believe that. I fought it, believe me. You've had me tied up in knots. When I looked at my little nephew this week I thought of you. Of us. Of the possibilities that might exist if—"

She finished his sentence. "Once you arrested my brothers and got that little item out of the way," she said bitterly. "There are no possibilities for you and me, Jude. None. Please leave."

Jude stood, looking at her for a long time. Then he turned and left.

Eleven

Three days later the four agents stood in the driveway of the home they'd shared for several months. Hal, John and Ruth waited for the cab they'd called to take them to the airport. Jude leaned against his sports car talking with them while they waited.

"I've enjoyed getting to know you guys," he said during a lull in the conversation. "I couldn't have asked for a better group to work with."

Ruth said, "I'm not sorry I'm getting out of this Texas heat."

"It's just as bad along the east coast, I can vouch for that."

John said, "Are you finally taking that vacation that was interrupted?"

"I'm going up to see the folks for a few days. I may go on back to Maryland after that and see if I still have my old job," he said with a grin. "If not, then I'll need to look for work."

Hal said, "You know where to come if that's the case, old man. Sam would hire you on the spot. He's pleased with what we've accomplished."

"I was glad to hear Davies and Sullivan spilled their guts to him. I'm sure they're hoping for a lighter sentence. Did they ever admit how your agent got killed?"

John shook his head. "If they did, we won't hear about it, but it may come out at trial."

"If it does, I'd appreciate someone letting me know."

Hal smiled. "Oh, don't worry about learning anything about the trial. You'll probably be asked to testify. In case you get homesick, know you'll be back here whenever this case is heard."

Jude nodded. "Thanks for the heads-up."

"There's our ride," Ruth said. "Take care of yourself, Jude."

"You, too," he said, and opened his car door. He waited until they had loaded their bags in the cab and driven away before he got in and slowly backed out of the driveway.

Jude had shipped most of his belongings to his office to await his return. Now he had nothing left to do but get out of town.

He didn't find the drive through the Hill Country as comforting as it had been in the past. His mind continued to race, replaying the last few days in his head. He tried to think of something he could have said or done to help Carina deal with all that had happened.

He hadn't been surprised at Carina's reaction. In fact, he'd expected it. There was probably nothing that would have made it more palatable for her once she knew that she'd been part of his assignment, although he had tried. He'd felt it important to tell her that what they'd had together wasn't part of this case.

She'd had too many shocks at one time to take in everything he'd told her. Even if she believed him she'd made it clear his role in her life was over.

He could only hope that sometime in the future she might look back and remember some of the good times they'd had together.

The problem he dealt with now was how much he missed seeing her. He'd known he would. He'd discovered that during the few days last week when he didn't call her. Knowing he would never see her again or hear her voice troubled him.

Of course he'd get over her, given enough time.

When Jude reached the ranch, he drove past Jake and Ashley's place without stopping and went to his parents' home.

By the time he pulled up beneath one of the cottonwood trees and got out, Joe's hunting hounds had him surrounded. He stopped and gave them some attention until he heard his dad whistle at them.

"That's enough, now, Blue. You, Benji and Buster give him some space." He watched Jude walk toward him. "Didn't expect to see you today. C'mon in." He held the screen door open and followed Jude inside.

"Where's Mom?"

"She's over at Jake's spoiling Joey, I imagine. She needed to run some errands, but she never goes past their place without stopping."

"I didn't see her car when I drove by, but I didn't stop, so she may have already been there and gone."

"She'll show up in a little while. Come on out back. There's a nice breeze out on the porch. You want something to drink?"

"Got any beer?"

"Most likely. I'll check. Go on out there and have a seat."

Jude stepped out on the porch and smiled. His dad had been whittling. He was getting really good at it, carving small figures of cowboys in caricature. This latest one wore an expression of disgust, his hands resting on his hips.

Jude stepped past his dad's rocking chair and side table and stretched out in one of the other rockers. He propped his feet on the railing and looked out at the view of the rolling hills. He was reminded of his first date with Carina, when they'd watched the sunset together. So much had happened since then that he found it hard to believe they'd known each other only a couple of weeks.

"Here ya go," Joe said, coming out the door. He held two longnecked bottles and handed one to Jude. "Might as well join you. Can you stay long?"

Jude sighed. "We're through with our operation in San Antonio, so I thought I'd visit for a few days. Then I need to get back to Fort Meade. I haven't been back to check on things at the condo for a month. I needed to stay in San Antonio once everything began to heat up. Hope I don't have any leaks or other unpleasant surprises waiting for me when I get home."

"You look tired."

"Haven't been sleeping much."

"Plus you look like you've lost your best friend."

Jude took a long swallow from his bottle. He swallowed and realized that his dad had pretty much described how he was feeling.

"I'm not surprised."

"Do you want to talk about it?"

Jude shrugged. "Nothing much to say. I met a woman as part of this assignment. We've spent most of the past two weeks together. We hit it off. I can't remember a time when

I've enjoyed a person more." He took another swallow. "And then last Saturday night I arrested her two brothers for smuggling dope."

Joe sat up abruptly, stopping his chair. "Did you know what they were doing when you met her?"

"Oh, yeah. That's why I was supposed to get to know her. As it turned out I didn't find out anything through her. Nothing. Nada. Zip. All our information came from other sources. At the end we realized there had been no reason to involve her, even peripherally."

"Damn. I take it she didn't like being set up and used."

"Among other things, yeah, that basically covers her reaction."

"Did she know about the smuggling?"

"No, but we didn't know that at first. If she'd been working with them, I would have found something on her. There was nothing."

"So it was necessary to date her, if for no other reason than to find out she wasn't a part of the operation. But you couldn't have known that, going in."

"No. I couldn't have. You're right about that. Wish that made me feel better."

"You really fell for her, I take it."

"I don't know what I feel about her. I just know I hurt her, despite everything I could do not to. I feel bad about that."

"The situation was set up where she would get hurt if she was an innocent party. If that was your assignment, you can't blame yourself for following orders."

"Well, it's done now. Once I'm back at work my life will get back in order and I'll forget her."

"Is that why you're not taking your vacation?"

"I'm taking a few days of it now. I may have to testify at the trial whenever it's set. I'll let you know when I'll be coming back." He grinned at Joe. "It'll give you an excuse to have a barbecue."

Joe nodded in agreement. "Good idea. We'll plan on it."

"In the meantime, I thought I'd fill up on some of Mom's cooking, laze around the house until you boot me out and maybe spend a couple of days with Jake and his men. It will remind me of why I don't like ranching," he added with a grin.

Joe picked up his whittling.

"What are you making?"

"This ol' fella's pretty upset. I'm going to carve his huntin' dog with feathers coming out his mouth. Won't be a pheasant he caught, but one of the old man's prized roosters, if I can do it. I want the rooster running away without his tail feathers."

Jude smiled. They sat in companionable silence for a while until he asked, "Have you talked to Jared recently?"

"He called last weekend. I'll call and tell him you're here. Maybe he and Lindsey can come over to visit with you."

"Is he settling in at headquarters all right or does he miss working out in the field?"

"I imagine he'd miss Lindsey more than he misses working in the field although he was never one for working inside. I wouldn't be surprised if he doesn't decide to do something else. Maybe hire out as a consultant to help others find oil. That way he could choose the jobs he wants."

"It seems strange that I've been so close to everyone and haven't seen much of anybody in the past six months."

"That's because you were working and the kind of stuff you do isn't like punching a time clock and having weekends off."

Jude laughed. "You got that right, Dad. You know something? It's good to be home."

* * *

Carina finished rehearsing, then put her music away before she left the school and walked toward the subway. It was now October and she enjoyed the pleasant temperature.

She hadn't wanted to come to New York after the arrests but her mom and dad had insisted that none of it had anything to do with her and she'd postponed her music education long enough.

She'd had no problem giving up her apartment. In fact, the week after her brothers were arrested she had moved back home.

The apartment held too many memories.

The place in New York she shared with two other students was nothing like her spacious apartment had been, which she appreciated. She didn't want any reminders.

Gloria, one of her roommates, had asked her this morning if she'd like to meet a friend of Frank's, Gloria's boyfriend, this weekend. Carina didn't much care. Maybe she'd go, just to change her routine.

After her divorce, Marisa had moved to Dallas to be near her family and bought a home but had returned for the trial to be with her in-laws during the ordeal.

Carina hadn't gone home for the trial. Her father had insisted she stay in New York and continue with her classes. She had, despite feeling guilty for her relief that she hadn't been there.

Marisa later told her that Jude Crenshaw had testified at the trial.

Carina hadn't asked about him. Marisa said he'd looked tired. She'd also reminded Carina that if her brothers hadn't been smuggling drugs, none of this would have happened, so why was she blaming Jude?

Marisa's question had been haunting Carina for several weeks. Her brothers were drug smugglers, the lowest sort of criminal she could think of. Marisa was certainly right about that.

What she had trouble accepting was Jude's pretending to care about her when he didn't. She'd practically thrown herself at him when he'd been reluctant to make love to her. How humiliating was that?

No. She was glad she'd never have to see him again. She didn't need the reminders of her one and only foray into seduction.

Just before she turned into the entrance to the subway she caught a glimpse of a man across the street who looked like Jude. At least he did at first. Same tall, rugged build and blond hair. But then he turned his head and she saw that of course it wasn't him. Jude wouldn't be in New York. He'd be working somewhere in D.C.

Her train appeared and she crowded on it, hanging on to a strap and wishing she were taller for, oh, maybe the millionth time. She waited until the next stop and when some passengers got off she found a pole to cling to.

She'd only known Jude for a couple of weeks and that had been at least three months ago and yet he still haunted her. He'd come into her life and jarred her fully awake as a woman. She'd trusted him. More fool, she. She doubted everything that he had told her about himself.

He probably wasn't even related to the Texas Crenshaw family. He could be from anywhere. He'd never offered to take her to the ranch he talked about. He probably didn't have a brother, much less a new nephew.

Well, maybe he hadn't lied about that.

Her thoughts were interrupted when the train drew into the next stop and she needed to get off.

She hated that her heart raced every time she spotted a

tall blond male. Jude wasn't worth one minute of her time. She wished there was a process where she could wash him not out of her hair but out of her brain.

As soon as she reached the apartment, she'd tell Gloria that she'd be glad to go out with her and meet Frank's friend.

"What happened to you while you were in Texas, dude?" Brad Johnson, one of the men Jude worked with, asked him one morning.

Jude had been typing up yet another report—was there ever an end to the damn things?—and glared up at him.

"You don't want to know," he replied caustically.

"Whatever it was, you've been taking it out on the rest of us since you got back. I figured you'd decompress and forget about it, but you've been a bear now for months."

"My Texas assignment is old history, long forgotten."

"Well, whatever is eating at you, deal with it, okay? If you don't lighten up around here there's going to be a lynching and you'll be the star attraction."

Jude closed his eyes and counted to ten. When he opened them, bright-eyed Brad still stood there.

"I was hoping I was hallucinating and that you didn't actually come in here and interrupt me while I'm trying to work."

Johnson backed away and paused at the door. "You know, Jude, work is tough enough without your bad-ass attitude to put up with as well, so whatever's going on with you, deal with it."

Jude saved the work he'd done and closed down the computer. He waited until he was sure Johnson would no longer be in the hall before he walked out of his office, his jacket tossed over his shoulder.

To hell with trying to concentrate; he was going home.

On the way to his condo he thought about the last few months, and knew that Johnson was right—he'd been in a foul mood and his co-workers had been forced to deal with him.

So face what's bugging you, Crenshaw.

He couldn't get Carina out of his head. She haunted him night and day. He could swear he heard her voice at times. Worse yet, he'd actually gone to a classical concert last week and was considering season tickets for the symphony.

If he ever decided to attend a ballet, he'd shoot himself because that would be a sure sign he'd gone over the edge.

So deal with it.

How? He'd never been so hung up on anyone in his life. He'd thought about calling one of his female friends to see if she wanted to go out, but he could never actually pick up the phone, much less key in her number.

He didn't want to see someone else. Carina had ruined his social life. It had never been all that great except when he'd taken on the role of playboy.

His work had always been his number-one priority and his social life lagged far behind.

Maybe that's all it was. He hadn't been to bed with anyone before Carina in too long for him to acknowledge without being embarrassed. If he hadn't been so hot for Carina right from the first time he'd laid eyes on her, he wouldn't have ended up in bed with her, either.

Deal with it. Get over it.

How?

Twelve

Carina knew she wasn't concentrating enough when she played the intricately fingered line of music several times and continued to make mistakes. She rested her hands on the keyboard and looked around the rehearsal room at Juilliard.

"I'm wasting my time. I might as well go home."

Carina packed up her music and left the rehearsal hall. It was Friday, the fourth of November, and the cold wind circled, blowing gusts of leaves and dust around her.

She buttoned her coat, raised the hood and started toward the subway. She'd left later than usual today. She would have nothing to do once she got back to the apartment, so she had stayed on and worked on one of her assigned musical compositions, for all the good it had done.

"Carina?"

Her hood blocked her peripheral vision and she stopped and turned. Oh, no. This time it really was Jude Crenshaw standing there in his secret-agent overcoat, his hands in his pockets and the wind ruffling his hair.

She didn't need this. She really and truly did not need this. She watched him walk over to her. She took a deep breath before she said, in what she considered a civil tone, "What are you doing here?"

He continued to look her squarely in the eye. Had his eyes always been so blue? He'd lost his tan, she noticed, and he looked thinner than she remembered him.

"Could we get coffee somewhere?" Jude asked. "I'd like to talk to you."

"I suppose. There's a deli in the next block."

He flashed a lopsided smile. "Sounds good. I'd like to get out of this wind."

She looked around the area. "How long have you been here?"

"A while."

"Mmm." Her last class had been two hours ago. Had he been waiting that long?

They walked to the light and eventually crossed the street. Neither of them spoke until they were seated and had ordered coffee.

"Are you hungry?" he asked.

She shrugged. "I suppose."

"We'll order when he comes back." He smiled into her eyes. "Nothing beats an authentic Reuben sandwich."

"Unless it's corned beef on rye." She knew she was sunk because, despite everything that had happened, and her determination to blot this man out of her mind, she was glad to see him.

What did that tell her about her state of mind?

There were lines around his eyes that hadn't been there last summer and the brackets around his mouth were deeper.

"Never underestimate the power of a really good Reuben." He didn't take his eyes off her. "You're looking good, by the way. School must be agreeing with you."

"My saving grace."

He didn't comment. Their coffee came and Jude gave the waiter their food order.

"So what are you doing here?" she said, once they were alone.

"I wanted to see you."

Not the words she wanted—or needed—to hear. Or maybe she no longer knew what she wanted or needed to hear. Her brain had turned to mush as soon as she'd seen him.

"Oh." Now there was a scintillating answer.

"Carina, I know how badly I hurt you—"

"Don't! Please. We don't need to discuss the past. It's over."

"I'm glad you feel that way because I'd like for us to start over. I've discovered something these last few months that I need to tell you." He paused and took a drink from his water glass.

Now that he'd gotten that far, he seemed to be searching for words. Carina realized she was holding her breath, waiting to see what he had to say that had caused him to come to New York.

She forced herself to exhale and reminded herself to keep breathing!

He met her gaze, looking grimmer, if that was possible.

"I'm in love with you," he said starkly. "I only recently discovered that. I think it happened at Crazy Eights, but I wouldn't swear to it. It may have been when you walked into the ballroom the first time I saw you, wearing a flame-red dress that's imprinted in my memory. I can't get you out of my head. I dream about you. I'm distracted at work. My co-workers are threatening to tar and feather me and run me out of town—if they don't lynch me first—because I've been unbearable to be around."

A muscle moved in his jaw as though he was clenching his teeth. Finally, he said, "This doesn't have anything to do with the case I was working on when I met you. I want us to forget the reasons why we met and look at how much we enjoyed each other during that time. I'm not in the habit of declaring my feelings like this." He grimaced. "Never have before, probably won't again. But I wanted you to know. I needed you to know. This is how I feel."

Carina felt as if she'd put her finger in a live socket when he said that he loved her. She felt a tremor race through her body, leaving her heart pounding in her chest. Whatever she'd expected him to say, "I love you" wasn't on the list.

She was speechless.

Doggedly, he continued, "I'm not asking anything of you except to consider what I've said. If you think there's a chance for us to have a relationship, you can let me know."

Their food arrived and Carina stared at the huge sandwich in front of her. She couldn't eat a bite. Not now.

Jude's appetite didn't seem impaired in the least. He was eating as if this was his first meal in days, possibly weeks.

Could he possibly be telling her the truth?

She didn't want to love him. She didn't want him in her life. She didn't trust him and she never wanted to be so vulnerable with anyone again.

When she finally looked up, there were tears in her eyes.

He paused and wiped his mouth, drank some coffee, and said, "I didn't mean to make you cry."

She bit down hard on her bottom lip. Finally, she said, "I appreciate your coming all this way to tell me, Jude. I just—" She blinked, then quickly wiped away a tear, "I don't think it's a good idea for us to try to pick up our relationship as though nothing had happened."

"I understand that. I really do. What I'm suggesting is a brand-new beginning for us. What if we just met today? Say a mutual friend introduced us. We could start today, right now, if you're willing. I know we won't be able to see much of each other and maybe that's better at the moment. We can talk on the phone, e-mail each other, share our deepest, darkest secrets…."

"I believe you know all of mine after the thorough investigation you did," she pointed out wryly.

"Then I'll share some of mine. What army life was really like, maybe, if you're interested. I didn't tell you the truth about my stint in the army. I enjoyed it. There was a camaraderie there that was tight as family. We were family…watching out for our buddies, working together. I couldn't tell you that before because that's where I got my training for covert operations."

"That's the problem, Jude. I don't know what the truth is where you're concerned. I don't know you. I don't think I ever did."

He cleared his throat. "If you're going home for Christmas, I'd like you to meet my family and show you the ranch where I grew up. Believe me, once you've spent any time around them, I'll guarantee you'll know everything about me—my most embarrassing moments and my less-than-stellar abilities as a rancher." He touched her hand briefly and pulled away. "I'm asking for a chance, that's all. I'd like you to get to know me when I'm not working, not pretending to be a playboy, not—"

"Whoa. Wait a minute. You were pretending to be a playboy?"

"'Fraid so. I don't normally have much of a social life."

"You definitely fooled me. You're very, uh, skilled." She could feel herself blush.

"Our intimacy was a whole new experience for me. I felt things I'd never felt before. I couldn't get enough of you." He chewed on his lip a moment. "I've never felt so intensely about anyone or wanted anyone so much…in my life, in my arms, in my bed, in whatever way you'll allow."

She fanned her cheeks. "It's awfully warm in here, isn't it?"

He glanced around. "Is it? I hadn't noticed."

She signaled the waiter as he came by. "Could you put this in a to-go box for me?" When the waiter left, she said, "I need to get home before dark. At the moment I don't know what to say or what to believe. I'll be honest. I don't ever want to hurt as badly as I did last summer. I'm not certain I can forget all of that."

He nodded. "I understand. What I'm suggesting is that we take it a step at a time. I'd like to call you once in a while. We can e-mail. You can respond or not, that will be up to you."

The waiter returned with the box and she quickly packaged her untouched sandwich. She found a piece of paper in her purse and scribbled the information he'd requested. "Thanks for supper," she said, and stood.

He stood and took her hand. "I'll be in touch."

She nodded and hurried away. Once outside, she glanced back into the deli. Jude continued to eat his sandwich as though everything in his life was normal.

She wished she felt the same.

As soon as Carina let herself into her apartment, Gloria greeted her. "Good. You're home. You don't have anything planned for tonight, do you?"

"As a matter of fact, I do." She placed her purse on a small table and put her sandwich in the fridge. "I need to call some friends and family. I've been too busy all week."

"Darn. Frank has a friend that—"

"Gloria. Stop. Frank has many wonderful friends. I know that. I believe I've met a great many of his friends. The truth is, I'm not interested in dating anyone." She took a deep breath and finally admitted out loud what she'd been refusing to face for months. "I'm still hung up on a guy I dated last summer."

Gloria's eyes widened. "You're kidding, right? I mean, you're just making this up so I'll leave you alone, aren't you? You've never, not once, mentioned a guy you dated last summer."

Carina sighed. "I know. I thought if I didn't talk about him, I'd forget him faster."

"Oohh. You really have it bad, honey. I never had a clue. And here I've been throwing one guy after another at you. Several of them really liked you and were disappointed when you wouldn't go out with them again. I just figured you were looking for Mr. Right. I had no idea you'd already found him."

She followed Carina into the bedroom they shared.

"I'm not saying he's Mr. Right," she said, changing into sweats. "All I'm saying is that I'm still hung up on him."

Gloria didn't say anything as she watched Carina change clothes. She followed Carina into the other room and watched as she heated water for tea.

"What's his name?" she finally asked, after several minutes of silence.

"Jude Crenshaw."

"Where's he work?"

"In Fort Meade, Maryland."

"How did you meet him?"

"We were both in San Antonio last summer."

"What happened that made you want to forget him?"

"It's too complicated to attempt to explain. My family was involved and the whole situation turned out to be a disaster."

"Like Romeo and Juliet?"

"Hardly. Anyway, I haven't seen or heard from him since June until today."

Gloria followed Carina when she carried her cup of tea into the bedroom and sat on her bed. Gloria sat down with a bounce on her twin bed. "Omigosh. You saw him today and you're just now telling me?"

"I could have come in and said, 'Oh, by the way, I saw Jude Crenshaw this afternoon.' And you would have said—?"

Gloria laughed. "I would have said, 'Who's Jude Crenshaw?'"

"Exactly."

Gloria went over and sat beside Carina. "You've got it bad, don't you?"

"That's a fair assessment."

"How's he feel about you?"

"If he's to be believed, he says that he's in love with me."

"And you don't believe him? Why?"

"Part of the long story. I'll work through it." She turned and faced her. "So where are you and Frank going tonight?"

Her question elicited a waterfall of explanations and exclamations, which gave Carina a break from being cross-examined. Her mind wandered back to their meeting. She had no idea what she would do. At least she didn't have to make a decision tonight.

Jude called Carina the Sunday afternoon before Thanksgiving. "How are you?" he asked when she answered the phone.

"I'm okay."

"You sound a little hoarse."

"Neigh."

"Ho-ho."

"I may be getting a cold. Nothing serious."

"Are you going home for Thanksgiving?"

"No. I'll be going after the semester ends in a few weeks."

"Same here. So. I was wondering if you'd mind if I came up there for the holiday weekend? I'll get a room, of course, but it would be nice to spend some time with you."

She'd enjoyed his e-mails. His wry sense of humor made her laugh, something that had been missing in her life. Maybe she'd been overly serious these past few months, but finding out that Al and Ben had been using the company to import illegal goods had devastated the entire family. A person didn't bounce back from something like that overnight.

"Okay. When do you plan to arrive?"

"Sometime Wednesday afternoon. I'll get a cab from the airport and call you once I check in. I thought you might enjoy seeing a Broadway show while I'm there."

"What? You won't take me to the ballet?" she asked, sounding astonished.

"Sure I will, if my snoring doesn't disturb you."

"I'll try to overcome my disappointment. I'm sure there are various things going on—such as Macy's parade—that will keep you entertained."

"Being with you will be entertainment enough."

"Jude…I'm not sure that…"

"Don't worry about it, okay? I do know how to be a gentleman."

She smiled. "Yes. I remember."

"I'll see you in a few days. Take care now," he said, and hung up.

He acted as though he'd never mentioned that he loved her. His e-mails had been casual and friendly. He wasn't pushing her at all. Her problem was being with him for several days without wanting to make love to him. His phone call had made her feel like a tuning fork, quivering at the idea that she would see him in a few days.

She had three days to prepare herself to be around all of that masculine energy without succumbing to him. She wondered if she could do it.

Thirteen

Jude checked in at the Marriott in central Manhattan a little after four on Wednesday afternoon. He'd pushed himself all week, working long hours to keep his mind occupied. Otherwise, he would have been imagining all kinds of scenarios about this weekend.

He'd had trouble sleeping last night. He'd tried but his thoughts had drifted into dreams of making love to Carina. He didn't need reminders, asleep or awake.

He shouldn't have told her he was in love with her. That had been a big mistake. She hadn't said a word in response. So he'd hurried on with other things he wanted to say. He was disgusted with himself for getting so deeply involved with her, with any woman. He'd been perfectly satisfied with his life until she came along. Now he found himself driving in the city, glancing at shops and movie marquees, wondering if Carina would like that living-room furniture or a particular bedroom set. Would she like to see that movie? He'd see a style of clothing on a woman and picture Carina wearing something similar. She might as well be in the car with him.

He'd lost his grasp on reality. What an idiot he was.

He'd thought about calling Jake to talk to him about what he was going through, but he didn't want to listen to Jake laugh. Had Jake gone through this with Ashley? Probably not, since they'd known each other forever. He sincerely hoped not. He wouldn't wish this emotional onslaught on his worst enemy.

Jude looked out the window of the hotel, glanced at his watch, and picked up the phone.

"Hello?" A husky voice cooed into the phone. He blinked. Had he gotten the wrong number?

"May I speak to Carina?"

"Oh! You must be Jude. Hi. I'm Gloria, Carina's roommate. Hold on and I'll get her."

When Carina picked up the phone, she was laughing. "Gloria says to tell you that she thought it was her honey, Frank, calling, and she apologizes for sounding so weird on the phone."

"She sounds like a fun roommate."

"You could say that, yes. Where are you?"

"At the Marriott. Are you up to going to dinner somewhere tonight?"

"Sure. Name the time."

"I'll pick you up at seven, if that's all right."

"I'll be ready." She paused and rushed out the words, "I'm looking forward to spending the next few days with you, Jude. 'Bye."

He hung up the phone, grinning. She sounded more like

the Carina he'd first known. He hoped the weekend helped to bring them closer.

Jude made dinner reservations and then went in to shower and shave. He felt as if it was his first date…in junior high.

He found a line of cabs parked in front of the hotel and gave the cab driver the address. Once inside, he sat back and forced himself to relax, glad he didn't have to drive in all this traffic.

When they pulled up in front of Carina's apartment building, he asked the cabbie to wait for him and then bounded up the stairs to the front door.

He checked for her apartment number and rang the buzzer.

"Jude, is that you?" He heard over the intercom.

"Yep."

"Wait there, I'm on my way."

When she opened the door a few minutes later Jude noted that Carina wore red tonight, a dress of cashmere with simple lines that hugged her figure. Did she remember what he'd said about— Of course she'd remembered. How many times had he mentioned his reaction to her in red? So she'd dressed to please him.

The thought gave him hope.

"Hi," she said, sounding breathless as she pulled on her coat. He helped her to adjust the collar and escorted her down the steps to the taxi.

Once inside the cab, he gave the address of the restaurant to the driver and turned to Carina. "How are things with you?"

"Couldn't be better. And you?"

Nothing like a stilted conversation to get the evening started. What next? The weather?

Carina mentioned school and he listened with interest

as she shared a few anecdotes about her classmates, making the stories light and amusing.

Later, during dinner, Jude had no idea what he ate because he was too busy asking questions and listening to her talk about her life as a child. He wanted to hear her stories, see her as a little girl and learn as much as he could about her.

Why? Because he was insane, obviously.

"I've been talking about myself all evening," she said after they'd finished their meal. "You haven't said much."

"You'll hear all about my childhood if you've decided to meet my family at Christmas. I told them that I hoped to bring you to meet them once we're back in Texas. Of course, you can decide not to go and I'll understand."

"Are you kidding? And miss out on all the stories about you?" She studied him for a moment. "I have a question for you. Do you really have an old army buddy back east?"

She was sorting through what he'd told her in an attempt to find what was truth and what was fiction. He didn't blame her. In fact, he understood.

He smiled at her, enjoying the way her eyes reflected the delicate flame of the candle between them. "You betcha," he said. "Several. We get together whenever we can find the time."

"*Those* are the stories I'd like to hear."

"You wouldn't hear any if you met them. We don't discuss the past. We did our jobs. Period. We don't look back."

She looked at him gravely. After a moment, she said, "I catch myself thinking about you as the man I knew last summer, which I know is wrong. Everything for you was pretense. I don't really know you, despite feeling so comfortable with you."

"What you need to understand is there was no pretense where you were concerned. There were things I couldn't discuss with you, but what I did discuss came from me and not the agent assigned to you."

"I wonder if the same thing would have happened if they'd sent someone besides you?"

He frowned. "I don't want to give any thought to the idea or I'd have nightmares. You once asked me if I was jealous. Yes, where you're concerned, but I'm working to overcome it. I'm not sure how to handle the possessiveness I feel whenever I look at you. I want to stand and shout 'I found her first, fellas. Eat your hearts out.'" He shrugged. "Even though I know I don't have the right to be possessive where you're concerned."

"How would you feel if I behaved the same way?"

He relaxed and settled back in his chair. "Are you kidding? I'd love it." He looked at her empty cup. "Do you want more coffee or are you ready to go?"

"I'm ready."

Jude kept his hand at the small of her back as they threaded their way through the tables and out onto the street. Once they were outside, they walked for a while, holding hands and looking into store windows. After several blocks, he said, "Are you getting tired? Are you ready for me to take you home?"

"Actually," she said slowly, "I'd like to see where you're staying."

He swallowed. "Yeah? Why?"

"No particular reason, I suppose. I'm not ready to leave you quite so soon."

"Is this a test of my willpower, because if it is, I've gotta warn you that it's getting a little shaky."

She stopped and turned to him. "I know you're kidding. You're too controlled ever to be swept away by emotion." She studied his expression for a moment. "I want to explore our new beginnings this weekend, Jude. As far as I'm concerned, you can let your willpower off the hook."

"Mmm. Now all I have to do is find a cab," he said, looking around at the heavy traffic. "I don't think throwing you over my shoulder and racing back to the hotel would be too smooth a move."

She laughed. He loved to hear her laugh. He loved watching her expressive face. He loved her.

When Carina had left her apartment that evening she'd had no intention of sleeping with Jude during his visit. Of course she'd missed being intimate with him. However, she recognized that her emotions were all over the place where he was concerned and she didn't trust her ability to make wise choices. The problem was that when Jude asked her if she was ready to go back to her apartment, she suddenly knew without a doubt that she didn't want to leave him. Not yet. Not so soon.

His response was so typical of Jude. He made light of everything. Almost everything. She'd noticed that he didn't joke about the way he felt about her. She still wasn't certain whether or not she wanted him to be in love with her. Knowing that made it more difficult for her to decide what she wanted from the relationship.

Now she'd committed herself to return to his hotel with him and her nerves were jumping. She was so vulnerable where he was concerned. She didn't know which was more painful, to spend time with him or not see him at all. Why had she thought when he suggested spending the holidays with her that she could remain detached?

They started walking toward the hotel. When one of the cabs he'd signaled saw him and pulled to a stop, Carina knew that miracles do happen: they'd gotten a cab on a very busy night.

Once at the hotel, Jude paid the driver and took her hand to enter the lobby. Once inside, she heard a live band playing in the lounge.

"It isn't country-and-western, but if the band is part of a lounge entertainment, maybe we could listen to some music," she said to Jude. She sounded breathless, darn it, when she'd wanted to sound blasé about the evening.

Jude wasn't fooled.

"Getting cold feet, are you?"

She glanced down at her shoes. "Well, it is November and I'm not wearing socks."

"That was really bad, you know," he said with a chuckle and slid his arm around her waist, pulling her to his side. "Whatever you wish to do, milady, I'm yours to command."

They started across the lobby. She glanced over her shoulder at him and smiled. "I'll remind you of that later."

The dimly lit hotel lounge was like a lot of places he'd been in during his travels. At least the music was better than most. They found a small table and sat, their knees bumping. He picked up his chair and moved to her side. "Now we can have some legroom." He casually draped his arm on the back of her chair.

The waitress took their order—wine and beer—and left.

"What would you like to do tomorrow?" he asked, hoping to sound casual.

"I don't care. Do you want to watch the parade?"

He played with a lock of her hair, rubbing its silkiness between his thumb and forefinger. "We could do that. You know the best place to watch it?"

"Not really. Where?"

"On TV, while lying comfortably in bed. The cameras give you close-ups that you wouldn't see if you were there, and you don't have to fight the crowds for a place to see."

"Mmm. It's obvious that you've given the matter considerable thought. Does that come with breakfast in bed?" she asked with wide-eyed innocence.

"That can be arranged with no problem."

She leaned her head against his shoulder.

Their drinks arrived. When the small group of musicians segued into a slow, romantic number he asked, "Care to dance?"

"Thought you'd never ask," she said with a sigh of contentment.

They danced three numbers before the band took a break. They returned to the table and Jude looked at his glass of beer—his glass of flat beer. Stale beer was worth the chance to hold Carina close, though, even though he couldn't hide her effect on him. He didn't try.

She touched her glass and said, "I really don't want this."

"Good," he said, standing. "I think it's time to retire, don't you?"

"I just remembered that I didn't come prepared for this…. No toiletries, nothing to sleep in…no protection."

"We'll get a complimentary toiletry package from the hotel. You won't be wearing anything, anyway, and I brought protection."

"You must have been a Boy Scout."

They left the lounge as he said, "As a matter of fact, I was for a while. As I recall, I got fired for pulling too many shenanigans. I believe it had to do with the beautiful badge I so carefully made representing rustling cattle or some such thing. The parting of the ways with the troop was one of mutual relief for me and our esteemed leader."

They stepped into the glass elevator. "Somehow that doesn't surprise me," she said, smiling.

When they reached his floor he strode down the hall and

paused in front of a door. Once he'd unlocked it, he held it open for her to enter.

The room was beautiful—roomy and exquisitely furnished. "Wow."

"My little home away from home."

She peeked into the bathroom. "A Jacuzzi, as well? How do you rate?"

"Must be my good looks and charm," he replied. The truth was he'd asked for a large room. He didn't mind the cost. He wanted to be comfortable for the four nights he'd be here.

He noticed the bedcovers had been folded back since he'd left and a chocolate kiss sat on his pillow.

He watched Carina wander over to the window and look out. He loved the view at night high above the streets and avenues of Manhattan. He loved it more with her in the foreground.

Jude removed his jacket and unbuttoned his shirt without taking his eyes off her. "Wanna get nekkid?"

She turned and gave him a delicious smile. Without replying, she reached behind her, unfastened her dress and slowly pulled it over her head. He almost lost it then and there, but forced himself to stay where he was and finish undressing. Once she'd laid the dress aside, he said, "Let me do the rest," and she obediently walked across to him in her lacy underwear and high heels.

He kissed her with all the pent-up longing he'd had for all these months. He stroked her lips with his tongue before dipping into the sweetness of her mouth. He paused only long enough to finish undressing them both and continued to kiss her as he sank onto the bed with her in his arms.

Jude took his time caressing her with his lips, his tongue and the pads of his fingers, slowly moving down her body until he reached her nest of curls. She was damp and ready for him. She took tiny, hitching breaths, responding to each touch, and moved restlessly beneath him.

He continued down her thigh, pausing to kiss and caress her knees and calves before slowly moving up the other leg.

"Please, Jude, please, please, please." She whispered the litany rapidly and he nobly obeyed her wishes…sliding deeply inside her. She dug her heels into his back and clutched him to her, meeting his thrusts and causing him to lose the little control that he'd managed to maintain. He'd wanted to go slowly, to savor her, but his need was too strong to be held back from completion.

She cried out at the same time he did, and it was some time before he could get his breath or do anything more than hold her tightly in his arms.

He kept his weight off her by balancing on his elbows. She stared up at him with those unfathomable eyes and he whispered, "What are you thinking? Or do I want to know?"

Her lips turned up at the corners. "I'd forgotten what it was like to make love with you."

"Hmm. Too many others to compare with these days?"

"No, of course not. I haven't had any interest in going to bed. With anyone. Until now."

"Glad to hear it," he said, and rolled off the bed. He went into the bathroom and closed the door. After he washed up, Jude returned to the bedroom. She lay on her side, her head resting on her hand, waiting for him.

When she saw him, she smiled and said, "I'd tell you what a gorgeous body you have, but it might go to your head."

As though he'd been celibate for years, his body leaped into life at her words. He glanced down and then up at her. "You could say that, couldn't you?" he said, before diving into bed and grabbing her.

Fourteen

The next morning Carina and Jude returned to her apartment to get her some clothes. They'd woken up early, but by the time they actually got out of bed and dressed, it was almost eleven o'clock. They made no pretense about the fact that she would stay with him while he was in New York.

When they reached her apartment on the third floor, he said, "No wonder you keep in such good shape, climbing those stairs."

"At least I don't have to carry a piano back and forth to school. Gloria carts her violin everywhere she goes. Not that she complains. We're just grateful to have been accepted at the school and that we found a place we can afford."

She stopped at their door and started unlocking it. After the third lock opened, she turned and said, "Welcome to my simple abode."

He walked in and turned in a circle. "Did you say three of you live here?"

"That's right. Annie went home to visit her family for the holidays and I imagine that Gloria stayed with Frank. She spends half her time at his place."

"I'm doubly glad I came to New York, then. You would have been here alone."

She went into her bedroom and gathered some clothes, slipping off her dress and putting on slacks and a sweater. "I'm used to it," she said with the sweater over her head. She felt like a turtle peeking out of its shell when she could see again.

"How much longer before you graduate?"

"I'll be finished next June. I haven't decided whether to continue with my education or look for a place where I can share my music with others."

He didn't comment.

She packed a dress to wear to the musical for which Jude had gotten tickets at an exorbitant price. They were attending the Saturday-evening performance. He'd be leaving late Sunday.

"Ready?" she asked him. He'd been wandering around the room, looking at the photos that Gloria had taped to her mirror and those that Carina had framed and set on her small desk.

He turned. "I'm always ready where you're concerned."

They returned to the hotel and didn't leave the room until Saturday.

As promised, Joe Crenshaw was having a barbecue. It was a week before Christmas. Everyone in the county had been invited and most of them generally showed up for a Crenshaw event.

The morning of the barbecue, Jude left the ranch early to pick up Carina in San Antonio. He hadn't seen her since Thanksgiving, although they'd stayed in touch daily by phone and e-mail.

They'd never discussed their relationship during their long weekend. It had been enough that she'd been willing to stay with him while he was in New York, and that she'd agreed to visit the ranch.

He knew she had little spare time, just as he knew she was very serious about her music. He wasn't certain where he might fit into all of this and didn't want to ask because he might not like the answer.

He drove into her parents' driveway at close to nine. Carina waited outside, near the front door. He got out of the car as she walked toward him. He wrapped her in his arms and held her tightly against him for a long, silent hug. When he released her, he took the small bag she held and placed it in the back seat, then helped her into the car.

"A new car?"

"No. It's one of Jake's. I'm using it while I'm here."

"Oh."

He started the car and turned to look at her. "What's wrong?"

"I'm not very good at hiding things, am I?"

"Not from me. Is it your parents?"

"Mom is very upset that I'm going with you today and more upset, if that's possible, that I'll be staying overnight. I explained that your sister-in-law had invited me to stay with them, but it didn't matter. She still blames you for all the unhappiness in the family."

Great. Just what he needed. He drove out of the driveway and headed north. After a few miles, he asked, "Does your dad feel the same way?"

She shrugged. "I don't know. He hasn't said much." She looked over at him. "Mother has already gone through so much that I hate to upset her more."

"And yet you decided to come with me, despite her reaction."

"I'd already told you I'd come with you and I've been looking forward to meeting your family. I finally had to tell her that I was sorry she felt the way she did, and because I was frustrated by this situation, I pointed out that you wouldn't have caused any unhappiness if Al and Ben hadn't been guilty of smuggling drugs!"

He was relieved to hear that Carina had defended him, but he hated the fact that her parents, at least her mother, felt so strongly about his role in the matter. He reached for her hand and said, "I'm glad you came with me. I would have been very disappointed if you'd cancelled."

Her hand felt cold. "Are you nervous?" he asked.

"A little."

"Please don't be. You'll meet Jake, Jared, their wives and Jake's kids and my folks. None of them bite, no matter what you may have heard about the Crenshaws."

"Thank goodness! That certainly relieves my mind."

He placed their clasped hands on his thigh. "However, I will warn you that they'll tease you unmercifully. The secret is to dish it right back at them."

"I'll do my best."

Two hours later they pulled onto the ranch road from the highway and Carina looked at the area in surprise. She'd expected to see a house or two near the highway. Instead she saw large pastures dotted with trees and shrubs.

They must have driven several miles before she saw signs of human life, but she'd seen several fields of longhorn cattle, sheep and goats along the way.

The house where they stopped was the size of a hotel and looked like an old-style hacienda. She sniffed. "What's that wonderful smell?"

"The meat Dad's barbecuing. He cooks it several hours before he considers it ready to serve." Jude helped her out of the car, took her hand and led her around the side of the house. A large patio filled a space between two wings of the house. On the patio there were three couples, a little girl and an infant.

The men stood as soon as they saw them. The older one stepped forward. "Welcome to our family home, Carina," he said with an attractive grin that immediately reminded her of Jude. He took her hand. "I'm Joe Crenshaw, Jude's dad." He turned and led her to the tables where the others watched. "This is my wife, Gail, the love of my life, my son Jake, his wife, Ashley, his daughter, Heather, and his son, Joey."

"You're pretty," Heather said, bouncing on her toes. "You look just like a doll my daddy gave me for my birthday. Want to see it?"

"Sure," Carina replied and watched Heather run into the house.

"This is my son Jared and his wife, Lindsey," Joe said, continuing the introductions. He turned to the family and said, his eyes dancing, "And in case you've been wondering why Jude's been acting so lovesick these past many months, here is the reason: Carina Patterson."

"Gee, thanks, Dad," Jude said. He'd let go of her hand when his dad met them, but now he reached for the other one.

She looked up first at one man and then the other. "They grow really tall Crenshaws in this part of the state, don't they?"

Ashley jumped up and hugged her. "Oh, yes! You're going to fit in just fine around here, honey. Come, sit down and have some iced tea with us."

"Hey, guys, I'm not really invisible. It just seems that way," Jude drawled, pulling up a chair for Carina and another one for himself.

The men sat down once Carina did. Jared looked at Jude. "Too bad you aren't invisible. Guess that means I have to look at your ugly face all day."

"You're confused, bro. The only ugly face you see around here is when you look in the mirror."

Carina kept looking at first one male and then the next. They were all gorgeous men...well-built, quick-witted and very sexy. She could appreciate their good looks and charm but her heart kept pumping in its normal way until she met Jude's eyes.

She blushed.

Gail said, "Don't let these guys embarrass you, Carina, this is the way they show affection for one another."

Everyone looked at Carina, and she knew she turned a brighter pink.

The door slammed and she heard running footsteps behind her.

Jake said, "She only has two speeds, you know—full-out and asleep."

Heather appeared at Carina's side. "Here," she said, thrusting a doll at Carina. She took it and smiled. It was a doll with long, dark hair, dressed in a colorful, Mexican-style costume. "Isn't she pretty?" Heather asked. "She's my most favoritest doll."

"That's true," Ashley said. "She wanted to sleep with it when she got it in September, but I convinced her to place it on a shelf at night so she could see it and not roll over on it."

"Uh-huh, 'cause I could break her and then I'd be sad."
She looked at Jude. "Did you bring Miss Carina for me,
Unca Jude?" she asked, her eyes sparkling with mischief.

Carina lifted her brows at Jude and waited for his answer.

"Actually, honey, I brought her for all of us to enjoy. I
agree with you. She's a beauty and so is your doll."

"Her name is Sophia," Heather explained, taking her
doll back from Carina. "You can play with her if you want."

"Thank you so much. Maybe later."

The next few hours flew by for Carina. She helped the
other women prepare a light lunch to hold everyone until the
barbecue; she rocked Joey while the others made huge
amounts of beans, potato salad and coleslaw. Later, she toured
the house with Heather as a talkative and delightful guide.
The best part, in her mind, was when the women told her stories about the Crenshaw males and how they'd met them. The
stories were hilarious and touching and highly informative.

She loved Gail's stories about bringing up four wild-
child males. Jude had been right. She was definitely hearing stories that didn't put him in a favorable light.

That evening she got a further glimpse into Jude's background when friends and neighbors showed up for the party. A band set up on the patio and several of the men moved
the tables aside for dancing.

She stood on the lawn some distance from all the activity and watched. Jude walked up behind her and slipped his
arms around her waist. "Think you can stand all this confusion for a few hours?" he asked and nibbled on her ear.

She turned her head and kissed him. "I'm amazed that
there *is* no confusion. Everyone has a specific duty, even
Heather, and they do it as though it's a routine."

"Oh, it's that, all right. I've lost count of the number of
parties Dad has thrown since I was born. I told him once

that if we didn't raise our own beef, he'd be broke buying supplies."

She turned to face him. "I like your dad, Jude. And your mom."

"I'm glad. They're both raving about you. Dad can't believe I have such good taste and Mom asked if you'd ever done any modeling. Both of them are wondering how I managed to get your attention."

"Do they know about my brothers?"

"Yes. I don't keep secrets from my family. What you have to understand is that your brothers' choices in life have nothing to do with you. I know you love them but the fact remains that if they hadn't been breaking the law, they wouldn't be in their present situation."

"I know. It's just so hard for my parents to accept."

"And I'm a constant reminder of their loss."

"I'm afraid so."

"I can live with that, Carina. I hope you can."

She sighed. "It was easier in New York, wasn't it?"

"Yeah, I guess it was. But the reality is that we both have family and they're a big part of who we are. We've got to face that and deal with it if we hope to have any sort of relationship in the future."

"I know," she said sadly. She stepped away from him. "I think I'll ask if I can help with something," she said, and walked away.

Jude watched her leave with an ache in his heart. He'd known that building any kind of relationship with Carina would be difficult, given their circumstances. He'd done his best to walk away from her until he discovered that he couldn't do it.

She might decide not to see him again and somehow he had to accept that possibility. He just didn't know how.

Fifteen

Carina had dozed off when she heard a quiet click that meant her door had opened. She turned over and saw a shadow moving toward the bed. In a low voice, she said, "I hope that's you, Jude, and not one of your brothers walking in his sleep!"

Jude sailed onto the bed, grabbing her and rolling, doing his best to muffle his laugh. He gave her a passionate kiss and her body melted like butter on a hot stove. When he finally lifted his head, he asked, "Recognize me yet?"

"I'm not sure," she mused. "You might want to kiss me again."

Their lovemaking was fast and furious and each of them experienced an explosive climax, leaving them limp and satisfied.

He stirred and muttered, "I have to go back to my room."

She played with his hair, pausing to say, "Poor baby, who sent you to your room?"

He rolled over onto his back and heaved a sigh. "As a matter of fact, Jake did. He told me if I absolutely had to be with you tonight, not to linger because Heather might wake up before we do."

"Ah, that explains the urgency."

"Naw, I was urgent because it's been weeks since I last made love to you and I've been suffering."

"Really. Suffering, huh? Are you out of your misery now?"

"For the moment." He caressed her face and shoulder. "Would you like to spend Christmas with us?"

"I'd like to but I can't. Mom and Dad wouldn't understand. They're doing their best to accept the fact that I'm seeing you again. Since I'll be their only child able to be home, I need to be with them."

He slipped his hand over her breast and teased her nipple. "I hope that in time things will ease between your parents and me."

"I called them after you left New York after Thanksgiving because I wanted them to know that I was seeing you again. I pointed out to them that if my brothers hadn't been breaking the law and smuggling drugs, none of this would have happened, that you had done the job you were hired to do."

"I'm glad to hear that you understand."

"It's taken me a while. I know the pain my parents feel and I suppose it's only natural they want to find someone to blame."

"When can I see you again?"

She thought about it before she said, "Let's wait. We'll both be going back east. Perhaps we should wait until then." He didn't say anything. Rather, he moved away so that he was no longer touching her. When he got out of bed, she said, "Jude?"

"I need to go. I'll see you in the morning." He pulled on his jeans and silently left her room.

Instead of going to his room, he went downstairs and out to the patio. Once most of the guests had left for home, the family had removed all signs of the party and replaced the table and chairs on the patio. He sat at one of the tables and stared at the sky. How had he ever gotten this messed up?

He needed to forget about her and get on with his life. Oh. Wait. He'd already tried that. He hated feeling so powerless over his life. Maybe it would be better for both of them if he stopped seeing her, toughed it out and stopped trying to build a relationship with her.

He didn't know how long he'd been outside when he saw the kitchen door open and Jake step outside. Like him, Jake wore jeans and was barefoot.

Jake sat down beside him and adopted Jude's posture—he slid down in the chair and propped his feet on the chair across from him. Jake didn't speak.

After several minutes of silence, Jude finally asked, "What are you doing up?"

"Got thirsty. You?"

"Figuring a way to get my life back. Carina's parents despise me. How's that for encouragement? I hate wondering if Carina will give in to her parents' pressure. I hate being in limbo—will she, won't she, does she love me enough to stand up to them or will she decide to settle for an affair until eventually she moves on."

"Did I ever tell you that Ashley refused to marry me when I finally asked her?"

Jude's head rested on the chair back and he slowly rolled

his head until he could see Jake's profile. "Uh, no, as a matter of fact, you didn't. She's been in love with you practically all her life. Doesn't make sense."

"Didn't to me, either, but it seemed perfectly logical to her."

"Women," Jude muttered. "You can't live with them, you can't drown them."

Jake chuckled. "True. Very true."

They fell into silence again.

Sometime later, Jake asked, "Have you asked her to marry you?"

"Nope. Hell, if she won't spend Christmas or New Year's with me, what would cause her to say yes to a proposal?"

"You're missing the point," Jake said. "Ashley and I are married now because we worked through what was bothering her. Bottom line, I hadn't communicated how I felt. If you don't, they don't have a clue where you're coming from."

"I told her I loved her."

"And?"

"And nothing. She just stared at me from across the table like she didn't understand English."

"Not too encouraging."

"You could say that. My only encouragement is that she's willing to go to bed with me, but that doesn't tell me much except she enjoys sex."

"Has she ever told you how she feels about you?"

"Not really. I guess she enjoys my company."

"She must care. She came to meet your family."

"Yeah, and then told me tonight that we should wait until we return east to see each other again, as though she's ashamed to be seeing me."

"You gotta admit the situation is highly unusual."

"I know. That's why I think we should forget about having a relationship."

"You'd be happy with that?"

"No. But I'm not happy now. Limbo sucks."

"What do you want to do?"

"Haul her off to a JP and marry her before she knows what happened."

"There's a reason Neanderthals no longer exist, bro. The women wouldn't tolerate their attitudes."

"You asked what I wanted to do, not what I would do, which is good, because I haven't a clue what I should do. The more I think about it, the more I think that breaking up is the answer."

"Your choice."

"At least I'm doing something."

"Even if it's wrong."

"Who's to say it's wrong? I want my old life back, the one before I ever laid eyes on her."

Jake yawned, stretched and stood up. "Lots of luck on that one, little brother. I'm going to bed."

Carina didn't see Jude when she went down for breakfast the next morning. Maybe he was still asleep. She found Ashley in the kitchen talking to a couple of women. She introduced them to Carina as the wives of a couple of the ranch hands who came in to do household chores.

"I have to go to the clinic," Ashley said once the women left the kitchen. "Thank goodness for preschool. That keeps Heather occupied. I drop her off each day and Jake picks her up at noon."

"Who keeps Joey?"

Ashley laughed. "Gail. She wouldn't hear of us hiring

someone. The woman who usually looks after the kids had
to leave for a while to take care of her sister who recently
had surgery. So this is a temporary arrangement." Ashley
looked around the kitchen. "Help yourself to whatever you
want to eat. We usually grab whatever's available most
mornings."

Carina poured some coffee. "Do you know if Jude's up?"

"Oh, he, Jared and Jake have been gone for the past couple of hours. No telling where they are, probably in the
barn. Jake's got a mare ready to foal. I told him she's
doing just fine but he's hovering. After that, it's anyone's
guess where they went." She lowered her voice. "Jared said
Lindsey wasn't feeling well this morning. It wouldn't surprise me to learn she's pregnant."

"The thing is, I really need to get home and I was hoping Jude would be ready to take me."

"Hold on." Ashley picked up the phone and pushed a
button and waited. After a moment, she said, "Hi, sweet-
ie. Is Jude with you? Oh, good. Carina wants to speak to
him." Ashley handed her the phone. "I've got to take Joey
to Gail's and get to work. It was so good to meet you, Carina. Please come back as often as you like."

"Hello? Hello?"

Carina realized that Jude was on the phone. "Oh. Sorry.
I was wondering when you could take me home?"

Silence.

"Are you ready to go?" he finally asked.

"Yes."

"I'll be right there." He hung up.

Carina went back upstairs and gathered her things together. Last night had been almost perfect. She and Jude
had danced, laughed, visited with other guests and been in
perfect harmony.

All that had obviously changed once she told him they should wait a while before seeing each other again.

What did he want from her? She didn't know. She supposed that if she wanted to find out, she'd have to ask him.

They were halfway to San Antonio before Carina broke the extended silence that had filled the car since they'd left the ranch.

"Jude?"

"Mmm?"

"Talk to me."

"About what?"

"Why you aren't talking to me for starters. Something's wrong. Has something happened with your family? Are you angry with me? I really dislike the silent treatment."

"Sorry. I've got a lot on my mind."

"Want to share?"

"I've been doing a lot of thinking and I've been wondering why you're bothering to see me if your parents are so against the idea."

She didn't answer right away. She knew she needed to be honest with him, but how could she explain the conflict between her head and her heart?

"I want to spend time with you," she finally said. "We've known each other six months. We can afford the time it will take for my parents to accept you in my life." She turned her head and looked at his profile. "I took you at your word last fall when you said you wouldn't push me, that we'd start over. Unfortunately, my parents aren't willing to start over. If you want to continue to date me, I think we need to see each other while we're on the east coast."

He gave a brief nod. "You're right. I promised not to push and now I'm pushing. I'm sorry. I want to continue to see you, regardless of what happens in the future." He looked at her, wearing a lopsided smile. "I wish I knew where I stand with you."

"I enjoy being with you, Jude. I believe that's been obvious."

"And?"

"And, what?"

"This is where you're supposed to give me some hope that I'm not the only one in love here."

She looked out the side window for a moment. "I miss you when you're not around. I think about you way too much. I dream about you. I would say that I'm besotted."

"You don't sound very thrilled about it."

"I wish I didn't have such conflicting feelings about you. It helped to meet your parents and brothers. You were right. I got a much clearer picture of who you are, being around them." She turned and looked at him. "It's too soon in our relationship for me to know if what I feel will last. I got too involved with you too quickly last summer and I paid dearly when I learned why you were pursuing me."

"I told you that—"

"I know," she said, interrupting him. "What happened made me realize how little I know about you. You had all of us convinced that you were a man with lots of money and no ambition."

"So what you're saying is, you fell for my cover persona."

"I suppose. If I could be so easily duped then, I know that I need to be much more wary now."

"Do you think I've been lying to you?"

"No. Not really."

"Do you believe that I'm in love with you?"

"I believe that you've convinced yourself of that, yes."

"Bottom line, you don't trust me or trust your own feelings."

"Yes," she replied in a quiet voice.

"Guess that tells me all I need to know."

Sixteen

Jude paced his living room.

It was late Sunday night and he'd just returned home from spending the weekend in New York.

"I've got to do something drastic or Carina and I will continue our long-distance relationship for the rest of our lives," he muttered. Great. Now he was talking to himself. Frustration was taking its toll on his sanity.

When he'd flown up to Manhattan on Friday, Jude made up his mind to ask her to marry him. It was April. He'd given her the time she'd requested to get her parents used to the idea that he was in her life. They'd had nine months to adjust. However, before he could bring up the subject Carina had mentioned that her parents, her mother especially, refused to discuss Jude whenever she called home.

So what was the point of proposing? Given the present

circumstances he knew what she would say and he didn't want her to turn him down.

Regardless of those circumstances, he didn't intend to give up.

Still pacing, he said, "This calls for drastic action on my part. She loves me, I know she does." He'd spent, on the average, one weekend a month in New York since January so that she could see that he was serious about her. She always greeted him with enthusiasm, which was about all that encouraged him these days.

An idea had formed on his way back to Maryland tonight that might move things along. He could go to Texas and speak to the Pattersons. Except for spotting them at the courthouse when he'd testified at the trial, he hadn't seen them since June.

So he would face them and listen to their objections. He hoped that he could convince them that he'd only been doing his job last summer and that he truly loved their daughter.

The thought of facing them called up emotions he hadn't had in years. He'd gone on dangerous assignments, jumped out of planes at night and faced enemy fire with an adrenaline rush that overcame his fear.

If he could handle those kinds of assignments, there was no reason for him to dread a confrontation with the Pattersons. At least they wouldn't shoot him.

He hoped.

He stopped pacing. All right. He could see that his next step had to be convincing Carina's parents that he really was a nice guy who happened to be head over heels in love with their daughter.

He could do that. He couldn't afford to fail.

With the decision made, Jude went into his bedroom and

stripped out of his clothes, then went in to take a shower. Standing under the spray of water he recalled his last shower. Carina had been with him.

He always stayed at a hotel when he was in New York and Carina stayed with him. She'd been lighthearted, counting the days until she finished her studies. The only time she grew quiet was when he asked about her parents.

He'd invited her to spend a weekend with him at his condo. He knew she'd love the area. The condo was large enough for the two of them. Once they married, they could buy a home.

He turned off the water and grabbed a towel. He could see their future together so clearly—if he could only convince her parents to give him a chance.

Once in bed he pulled one of the pillows to his chest, went to sleep and dreamed he held Carina in his arms.

Jude caught an early plane the following Saturday. He'd debated with himself all week about telling Carina or her parents that he would be visiting them.

He'd finally decided against the idea. Her parents would be less likely to dismiss him if he were there in person. He knew that Carina would hear about the visit sooner or later and decided he preferred the news to reach her later.

She might try to talk him out of it. She might actually persuade him not to go. The fact was, he was nervous about the trip. Hell, he'd rather be bailing out of a plane, or shot at than to meet with the Pattersons. After all, it was only his future they'd be talking about. He had no idea if he'd be allowed inside their home, much less get the opportunity to sit down with them and discuss his situation.

Once he landed in Austin, he rented a car and drove to their home.

The trip wasn't nearly long enough for him to calm his nerves and prepare for who-knew-what kind of reception.

Helmuth opened the door at his knock.

"Good morning, Helmuth. Are Mr. and Mrs. Patterson home?"

"Yes, Mr. Crenshaw." He turned away. "I'll tell them you're here."

Jude stood and waited. He recalled the time last summer when he'd thought he'd never see her again and the courage it had taken him to fly to New York to talk to her. He'd been nervous then but he'd gotten through it. He was here now and he needed to plead his case, if only they would listen.

"This way," Helmuth said from the back of the foyer. As Jude approached, Helmuth directed him to the doorway to a beautiful room with two walls of glass. The room was filled with tropical plants, and there was a garden outside the room that seemed to be part of the garden inside.

Chris Patterson sat in his wheelchair with his back to the room, facing the garden outside. When Jude paused beside him, Chris slowly turned his head and met Jude's gaze. "So you came." He turned his chair to face Jude, nodding toward a nearby chair. "Sit down and tell me why you're here. I assume you want to discuss Carina."

Jude took the chair indicated and sat. "Yes, sir."

"All right. Talk."

All the thoughts and phrases he'd rehearsed for the past week left him and for a moment his mind was blank.

He coughed. "I'm in love with Carina."

Chris didn't change his expression. "In my opinion, to know her is to love her."

"I agree."

"However, you betrayed her trust in you and hurt her terribly. All three of our children were caused enormous pain because of you."

Jude leaned forward and rested his elbows on his knees. "With all due respect, sir, if your sons hadn't been smuggling drugs, none of this would have happened. I would have been delighted to find that they were innocent because I knew what would happen if they were guilty. I believe you know that it was your sons who created so much grief. I was there as part of my job. I didn't frame them, nor was I particularly happy when I had to arrest them."

"I understand you don't work for the DEA."

"No, sir. I was asked to work on this particular assignment because of my background."

"So you lied to my daughter and pretended to have an interest in her. You said at the trial that meeting her was part of your assignment."

"Meeting her was part of my assignment, that's correct. Falling in love with her wasn't."

"You hurt her badly."

"Yes, sir, I know. I can't tell you how much I regret the necessity of not telling her the truth. But I couldn't, for obvious reasons."

"My wife refused to see you today."

Jude nodded. "I can understand that. No amount of logic can change the fact that she's suffering because your sons are in prison. I hope that eventually she'll realize that whether I was the one to arrest them or someone else, the end result would have been the same."

"Is this why you wanted to speak to us?"

"Partly. I came in hopes that you and your wife might be willing to accept me as part of Carina's life, because I want to marry her."

"Ah."

Jude didn't know what else to say.

Chris waited before he said, "Does she know that?"

"On some level, I'm sure she does. If you're asking whether I've asked her or not, the answer is no because she won't discuss the possibility of our having a future together until you and Mrs. Patterson accept me as a prospective son-in-law."

"You have quite a reputation for being a ladies' man. Is your interest in her because she may be unattainable?"

"My reputation was part of the role I was assigned to play. I believe I've convinced Carina that I'm far from a ladies' man. I've never had much time for a social life, either while I was in the military or later."

"Are you asking permission to propose to Carina?"

Jude replied, "In a manner of speaking, yes. Without your acceptance of me, Carina and I have no hope of planning a future together. She loves and respects you and Mrs. Patterson too much to ignore your feelings."

Chris sighed. "She's always been one to put us first in her life. By the time I discovered she'd left school and come back to San Antonio after my stroke, it was too late to insist she stay in school." He studied Jude for several minutes in silence. "I admit that when you took her to meet your family last December I knew you were serious about her."

"Yes, sir. I am."

"She didn't want to discuss you with us, partly because she saw how upset Connie became when your name was brought up. The fact of the matter is that I don't know anything about you other than your name and that you work for the government. I believe that Carina cares for you, given the way she grieved when she found out your meeting with her was premeditated. Why don't you stay for lunch and give me an opportunity to find out more about you?"

Jude took a deep breath and released it with something like relief. He didn't care how long Chris Patterson chose to grill him. At least he was speaking to him. He'd cleared the first hurdle.

Classes were over except for final exams. Carina stared out her bedroom window and thought about the last year. So much had happened in her life, both good and bad.

Jude came in somewhere in the middle. She was glad she'd met him and sad for the circumstances surrounding that meeting. The revelation about her brothers had been horrible to face. Life went on, though, and she needed to concentrate on today and stop looking back at yesterday.

Thinking of Jude, which she often did, she had been disappointed when he'd e-mailed to say he wouldn't be able to visit her this weekend.

Despite everything, she'd fallen deeply in love with him and knew that if he walked out of her life, she'd be devastated. Her feelings for him were nothing like what she'd felt for Danny. Jude was much tougher than Danny. Jude's life experiences had hardened him…and yet he'd always been gentle and loving with her. She found it more and more difficult to tell him goodbye when he had to return home. But…how could she find happiness with a man her parents disliked so much? She would be in the middle, wanting to be with Jude and wanting to be with her family.

Carina looked around the small room. She needed to begin packing her things in preparation for moving back to Texas. She'd find herself a nice apartment and do what she could to convince her parents that Jude was a wonderful man who made her very happy.

The phone rang a half hour later and she dropped the handful of clothing she'd taken from the closet to the bed.

"Hello?"

"Hi, baby, how's my girl?"

She sank onto the side of the bed, smiling. "Hi, Daddy. I'm doing great. How about you?"

"About the same. I had a visitor a couple of weeks ago."

"Oh? Did Aunt Lauraine decide to visit you?"

Her dad chuckled. "No. The last time I heard from her, she was on her way to Europe for an extended stay. No, Jude Crenshaw came to see me."

She felt the shock throughout her system. "Jude? Came to see you? Why?"

"I think he wanted me to get to know him a little better. He was very forthright about his reasons, I must admit."

"And they were…what?"

"He wants to marry you."

Carina appreciated the fact she was already seated. "He went to see *you* when he's never asked *me?*"

"He didn't want to risk being turned down, from what I gathered. He seems to think that you put our happiness before yours."

That was insulting and it irritated her. "Where would he get such an idea?"

"From all indications, he got it from you. He said you wouldn't talk about the future with him because of our feelings toward him."

"For your information, I don't put your happiness before mine. I'm thinking of my happiness and I wouldn't be happy if you were against my choice for a husband, so he's wrong there."

"Guess I phrased it wrong, honey. He didn't actually say that, but from where I sit, that appears to be what you're doing."

She wasn't sure what to say.

"Carina?"

"I'm here. I'm still adjusting to the fact that he came to see you."

"He gave me permission to have him investigated in case I had doubts about the kind of man he is."

"And did you?"

"Nope. I figure there's nothing there that I'd dislike, otherwise he wouldn't have suggested it. My question to you is, are you in love with him?"

"I've fought it for a long time, but yes, Dad, I'm definitely in love with him."

"Then you shouldn't let anyone come between you. Yes, your mother and I had bad feelings toward him, there's no denying that. Your mother still does, but I think that eventually she'll come around. You may think that you'd be unhappy marrying him without our blessings, but if you don't marry him, you'll come to resent having given him up for us."

"Oh, Dad! I'd never resent you. How could I?"

"I want you to follow your heart. I believe that your mother will come around eventually, especially if Jude becomes the father of her precious grandchildren. It will take time, though. I won't try to sugarcoat her feelings. She can't separate him from the pain she feels for Ben and Al."

"They were proven guilty, Dad. They were smuggling drugs. Doesn't that bother her at all?"

"Of course it bothers her, but it doesn't mean she can stop loving them. She lost her grandchildren as well when Marisa and Sara moved away from San Antonio. What happened turned her life upside down."

"Why blame Jude?"

"Because she needs to blame someone other than her sons."

Carina paused before she said, "That doesn't make sense."

"Exactly. You shouldn't allow her attitude to sway your decision to marry him. You're a grown woman with a bright future ahead of you. If you want my advice, I'd say don't let this man go. If you do, I know you'll be sorry."

She swallowed around the lump in her throat. "Thank you for calling to tell me that. Now all I have to do is wait for him to propose."

"You've got time, sweetheart. Know I love you and want to see you happy for all the right reasons."

"Tell Mom I love her."

"I will."

"Does she know you called?"

"Of course. We don't keep secrets from each other, even when we don't always agree."

"I love you," she said, fighting tears.

"Same here. We'll talk soon."

Carina hung up the phone and stared blindly at the instrument. She'd needed that phone conversation so much. She was sorry to upset her mother but her father was right: she couldn't make life decisions for herself on the basis of her mother's feelings.

She looked at her wall calendar, where she'd marked the time and date of her finals. She would be through Friday morning. She picked up the phone and made reservations to fly to Maryland Friday afternoon.

For some reason the rush-hour traffic was worse than ever for a Friday. Probably everyone was leaving to spend time in the country to enjoy the spring weather.

Jude might decide to do the same. He had household chores to do in the morning but after that, he might take a drive.

He hadn't heard from Carina this week, which wasn't a good sign. Had her father told her about his visit? Could she be angry because he hadn't told her he was going?

He didn't know what to think, since she hadn't answered any of his e-mails this week. Maybe he'd call her tonight. If she refused to speak to him, then he'd know he'd really blundered.

Eventually he reached his neighborhood. Thank goodness traffic had thinned out. He hit the garage-door opener as he turned into his driveway, and a movement at his front door caught his eye. He looked and saw Carina, who must have been seated on his steps because she had risen as soon as she saw him.

He stopped the car before pulling into the garage and got out.

Carina walked over to him, smiling. "I decided to take you up on your invitation to visit," she said.

"I can't believe this," he said in wonder. "I haven't heard from you in a week. I didn't know how to interpret that and now you show up on my doorstep." He grabbed her and held her close. "I've missed you so much!" he added and kissed her with passion.

When she pulled away from him, she was laughing. "Your neighbors are watching."

Without looking away from her, he said, "Let them eat their hearts out. How long have you been here?"

She glanced at her watch. "About ten minutes or so."

"Have you eaten?"

"Not since lunch."

"Let's get your bag inside and I'll take you to dinner. I can't believe you're actually here."

With his arm around her shoulders, he led her to the garage and into the kitchen. Then he went to the front door and opened it to get her suitcase. When he returned he found her in the living room. "Oh, Jude, this is so nice. How long have you lived here?"

"Almost four years. I'm not here all that much." He started upstairs. "Come see the rest of it."

She paused at the top of the steps. "How many bedrooms?"

"Two."

"They must be huge."

She followed him into his bedroom and peeked into the bathroom. "Oh, this is beautiful."

"Glad you like it."

She turned to him and he suddenly realized that she was nervous and trying hard to hide it. Why? Did she actually think he'd be upset to see her?

He walked over to her and cupped her face in his hands. "Have I ever mentioned that I love you?" he asked softly.

"Maybe a time or two, but I never get tired of hearing it."

"Good." He kissed her, putting everything he felt for her in the kiss. When he finally lifted his head, they were both trembling. "I've never heard you tell me how you feel about me, you know."

She paled, a reaction he hadn't expected, and he frowned.

"Do you honestly believe I would have gone to bed with you if I didn't love you to distraction?" she replied. "I tried to convince myself at first that you were someone to date until you grew tired of me. But it was more than that. Much more. I've never felt so much love for anyone as I feel for you."

Jude's heart seemed to swell with her words. He'd hoped, but hadn't been sure. "Are you talking about the evening you seduced me?" he asked her, teasing.

She blushed. "I was hoping you'd forgotten that."

"I've forgotten nothing about you," he said, and proceeded to slide each item of clothing from her until she stood before him in all her unclothed splendor. Then he lifted her and placed her gently on the bed. He removed his clothing in record time and lay down beside her. He cupped her breast in his hand and said, "You are so beautiful."

She ran her fingertips across his chest. "You make me feel beautiful, Jude."

He took his time making love to her. He kissed and caressed her all over her body until he could no longer stand not to be inside her. As soon as he moved over her, she wrapped her arms around his neck and locked her legs around his hips.

He didn't rush his entry; instead he continued to kiss and stroke her. She gasped when he pulled one of her nipples into his mouth, keeping his rhythm slow and easy until she lifted her hips in an effort to make him move faster. He chuckled and rolled until she was on top, and then he encouraged her to set their pace.

Jude let her move over him until he could no longer hold back. He held her hips while he moved in an escalating rhythm that brought both of them to an explosive climax.

She collapsed against him and he slowly stroked her back, following her spine from top to bottom and back up. Her hair spilled around them and he ran his fingers into its silkiness.

He didn't know how long they lay in that position until she shifted and slid off him. He turned to face her, drinking in each feature. He was still finding it hard to believe that she was actually here in his bed.

Carina slowly opened her eyes and smiled at him. He smiled back. "I've been meaning to ask you," she said. "When do you intend to make an honest woman of me?"

He froze in shock for the barest minute before he said, "You mean it? Will you marry me?"

She placed a light kiss on his mouth and replied, "I thought you'd never ask."

He grabbed her, held her as tightly as he could without crushing her and laughed, feeling the joy well up from deep inside. "Well? Will you?"

"Yes."

"Today? It's too late for today. Can you stay over until Monday?"

She chuckled. "Actually, I was thinking more like June, say on the date I first met you. What do you think?"

"Two months. I'm not sure I can hang on until then."

She kissed him again. "I have faith in you, Mr. Crenshaw. You'll manage just fine."

Epilogue

Once again, the Crenshaws had cause for yet another celebration. Jude and his bride, Carina, had been married earlier in the day at the ranch and now all their friends and family were there to wish them well at one of Joe's famous barbecues.

When Jude had asked her if she wanted to be married in San Antonio, Carina had said no. The notoriety caused by her brothers' arrests and trial had taken its toll on the privacy of their family. So Jude suggested they be married at the ranch, as his brothers had been. Joe and Gail's sons seemed to have started yet another tradition for the Crenshaw clan.

Earlier in the day when Jude went to stand beside the pastor before Carina joined him at the altar, he was glad to see Mr. and Mrs. Patterson in the small group attending the wedding. Connie looked as though she'd rather be anywhere else, but at least she'd come for Carina's sake.

Now it was time to celebrate and if there was one thing the Crenshaws knew how to do, it was how to throw a party.

Jude and Carina sat at one of the picnic tables—after she'd changed out of her wedding gown—and watched the crowd swirl around the food on several laden tables.

"I'm sorry your parents left so soon after the wedding," he said, raising their clasped hands to his mouth and placing a kiss on the back of her hand.

"Dad said that he'd promised Mom if she'd come with him, they wouldn't have to stay and pretend to be happy about the marriage."

"Whatever the reason, I'm glad they came."

"Me, too. Dad believes that eventually she'll come around and told me not to give the matter any more thought. He said we're welcome to come visit anytime."

"Hey, you two," Jake said, walking over to where they sat. "You'd better get something to eat or Dad will think you don't like his cooking."

"Sure he will," Jude replied, grinning. "As if he's noticed who's in line and who isn't."

Jake sat across from them. "It's good to see you so happy, bro." He looked at Carina and added, "Thank you for rescuing the family from having to look at his long face. Boy, he was a basket case over the Christmas holidays. I figured we might have to shoot him to put him out of his misery!"

Carina nodded graciously. "Of course, that's the only reason I decided to marry him, for the family's sake." She ruined her solemn pronouncement by chuckling.

"When do you have to go back east?" Jake asked.

"Not until after the fourth of July," Jude replied. "I guess my boss and co-workers are just as relieved I finally got

married as you are. They gave me a party with a bunch of
gag gifts and I was told to take an extra week off."

Jake laughed. "I'm not surprised, if you've been anything at work like you were here last winter."

"I wasn't *that* bad, was I?" Jude asked, his eyebrows
drawing together.

"Yep, you were, so congratulations again for finding the
love of your life. Wasn't it about a year ago that you were
telling me you had no intention of getting married?
Mm-mm. How the mighty have fallen."

Their mother walked up in time to hear Jake's remark.
"Actually, I've heard that same statement from each of my
sons and look at the three of you now. Domesticated. Who
would have believed it?"

Heather came running over to her daddy to tell him
something really important before she dashed away to be
with her friends. Carina smiled. "She's such a doll."

"When she's asleep," Jake added.

Jude looked at his mother. "I haven't heard anything
from Jason. Does he even know that I was getting married?"

"I don't know if he got my e-mail or not. I haven't heard
from him in several weeks, which always worries me. His
work is so hush-hush that I never have any idea where he
is or what he's doing."

Jake stood and said, "C'mon, y'all, let's eat. I, for one,
am starving." He looked at Jude and said, "And you need
to keep up your strength."

Carina blushed and laughed while Jude helped her up
and shot a cool glance at his brother. "Has anybody told
you what a wit you are?"

"Nope."

"Not surprising."

After everyone had eaten, the band began to play. Jude

took Carina's hand and led her onto the cleared patio. He took her in his arms and began to move to the slow love song. "Do you remember the song?" he asked.

"I've heard it, if that's what you mean."

"This was the song that was playing when I asked you to dance the night we met."

"Oh. So you asked them to play it for us."

"Um-hm."

She rested her head on his chest. "Sometimes I have trouble reconciling the fact that the tough government agent and the oh-so-romantic man I know are the same person."

"I gotta admit, it surprises me, too. My army buddies would be laughing their heads off if they could see me now."

She stopped and rested her hands on his cheeks. "I know the agent is skilled and does his job admirably, but it's the romantic who stole my heart."

* * * * *

*We hope you enjoyed DOUBLE IDENTITY,
the third book in Annette Broadrick's bestselling
Desire series, THE CRENSHAWS OF TEXAS.
Please look for the story of Jason, the youngest
Crenshaw brother, in the fall of 2005.*

Brenda Jackson

and Silhouette Desire present a hot new romance starring another sexy Westmoreland man!

JARED'S COUNTERFEIT FIANCÉE

(Silhouette Desire #1654)

When debonair attorney
Jared Westmoreland needed a date,
he immediately thought of the beautiful
Dana Rollins. Reluctantly, Dana fulfilled
his request, and the two were somehow
stuck pretending that they were engaged!
With the passion quickly rising between
them, would Jared's faux fiancée turn
into the real deal?

Available May 2005 at your favorite retail outlet.

If you enjoyed what you just read,
then we've got an offer you can't resist!

Take 2 bestselling
love stories FREE!
Plus get a FREE surprise gift!

Coming in May 2005
from Silhouette Desire

DYNASTIES: THE ASHTONS

**A family built on lies...brought together
by dark, passionate secrets.**

Nalini Singh's
AWAKEN THE SENSES
(Silhouette Desire #1651)

Charlotte Ashton was quiet and shy, but to
renowned winemaker Alexandre Dupre, she was
an intriguing challenge. Charlotte's guarded ways
had him wanting to awaken her senses, and pretty
soon Alexandre was too tempting to resist.

Available at your favorite retail outlet.

COMING NEXT MONTH

#1651 AWAKEN THE SENSES—Nalini Singh
Dynasties: The Ashtons
Charlotte Ashton was quiet and shy, but to renowned winemaker
Alexandre Dupre, she was an intriguing challenge. Charlotte's
guarded ways had him wanting to awaken her senses, and pretty
soon Alexandre was too tempting to resist. Yet, Charlotte didn't just
want a fling—she wanted him forever.

#1652 THE TEMPTING MRS. REILLY—Maureen Child
Three-Way Wager
Brian Reilly had just made a bet not to have sex for three months,
when his stunningly sexy ex-wife blew into town. It wasn't long before
Tina had him contemplating giving up his wager and getting her back.
But the tempting Mrs. Reilly had a reason of her own for wanting Brian
to lose his bet...to give her a baby!

#1653 HEART OF THE RAVEN—Susan Crosby
Behind Closed Doors
When private investigator Cassie Miranda was assigned to find a
mysterious baby, she never thought she'd have to help out his
dashingly handsome father. Reclusive businessman Heath Raven
was hardly prepared to become a dad, but Cassie saw a man with a
hardened heart that she was all too willing to soothe.

#1654 JARED'S COUNTERFEIT FIANCÉE—Brenda Jackson
When debonair attorney Jared Westmoreland needed a date, he
immediately thought of the beautiful Dana Rollins. Reluctantly,
Dana fulfilled his request, and the two were somehow stuck pretending
that they were engaged! With the passion quickly rising between them,
would Jared's faux fiancée turn into the real deal?

#1655 ONLY SKIN DEEP—Cathleen Galitz
To put an end to her single status, Lauren Hewett transformed from shy
bookworm into feisty bombshell while her former crush, Travis Banks,
watched with more than passing interest. Travis wasn't exactly looking
to lay his heart on the line but Lauren wasn't interested in an attraction
that was only skin deep....

#1656 BEDROOM SECRETS—Michelle Celmer
Ever since that one time Tyler Douglas had trouble "performing" in
the bedroom, he'd been too terrified to even be in the same room with a
woman. So when he offered to let the beautiful Tina DeLuca stay in his
home, he did all he could to keep her out of his bed. But Ty was more
than Tina would—or could—resist....

SDCNM0405